# FAKE SUMMER WIFE

## HALEY TRAVIS

# 1

## CLAUDIA

People always went on at length about how much they hated Mondays, but I loved them. It felt like I was getting a fresh start. Monday was the day to plan everything that would happen during the week, and discover what lay ahead.

Mondays were full of possibilities.

I wanted to believe that I was full of possibilities as well. After a full day of schoolwork, I rushed to my job as a waitress at Ray's Diner. It was a great place, and the evenings were relatively steady. I still had two more college courses to complete, and in addition to some freelance writing, I worked Mondays, Wednesdays, and Thursday nights at the diner. The tips did a lot to supplement my tiny income.

When I started here last year, I didn't even know if that was going to be possible. How could a girl who was naturally shy show enough personality to earn real tips?

But I dug deep, and drew on the acting classes I had taken in high school. "Claudia the waitress" was the bubbly, sometimes cheeky hit of the diner.

It made everything so much easier. If there was something wrong with an order, I simply made terrible fun of Scotty, our cook, causing him to come to the pass-through and shake his fist at me in mock anger. Customers loved it when we joked around, and would forgive any small mistake. Although now that I'd been working here for almost a year, everything was smooth sailing.

Ray, the owner, was only here during the day when it was busiest, and he trusted me enough now to leave the second I arrived so he could get home to his new baby.

I was actually going to miss the diner when I started a full-time job in October. With six weeks of summer left, I was hoping to find just a bit of excitement.

Dashing into the restaurant with ten minutes to spare, I used the back door to cut through the kitchen to the staff changing area.

I didn't like customers seeing me when I wasn't in my uniform. Somehow, the separation between my public self and private one was more defined that way.

Once I was in my blue and white dress with my hair tied up in a ponytail, I stuck my head into the kitchen. Diane, the daytime waitress, waved from the other side of the pass-through.

"Your boyfriends just sat down," she said with a wink.

She disappeared with two plates of food as Scotty looked over his shoulder from the grill with a raised eyebrow. "Those guys eat like horses. Are they good tippers at least?"

"Yes, absolutely," I said. "Everything good in here?"

"Yeah – get out there before they start chewing on the seats."

I tied on my apron, grabbed menus, and headed out to the two huge construction workers in the end booth. They'd been coming in for the past few weeks, and I liked them a lot. They were great, hard-working guys who loved to tease everyone and get them laughing.

As soon as I reached their table, I stepped away with the back of my hand against my forehead. "Good Lord. I knew that my gentleman friends would be coming in to see me today. Must be my psychic powers."

Taylor laughed loudly, as he always did, making the elderly patrons by the front door turn around and shake their heads in bemusement.

Bob reached over to give him a smack on the arm. "Pipe down. Don't freak out the normal people."

"I'm sure you're not including yourself amongst the normals," Taylor laughed just as loudly as he had before.

They were both broad-shouldered men, at least six foot one or two, with sandy brown hair. I had pegged them as brothers the first time I served them.

I handed them the plastic laminated menus, not without bopping them both on the heads first. "You boys are going to settle down for me, right?"

"Yes, Ma'am," Taylor said, rolling his eyes.

"We have to settle down today," Bob said. "And we'll need another menu. Our boss is on the way."

"Sure thing."

I brought them another menu, and three glasses of ice water, smiling to myself as much as to them. It would be fabulous if more of their friends and coworkers could start coming in on my shifts. Great guys, great tippers. Plus, it was nice to have a few more people to talk to. The seniors mostly kept to themselves at the other end, and the late night coffee and laptop crowd wasn't very chatty.

I'd only moved back to Kingsville last year, and my friends had scattered to the four winds. School, relationships, families moving around...people didn't tend to stay in one place these days. It was proving hard to build up friend-ships again, especially when I was naturally a bit timid around new people.

After pouring another round of coffee for two tables near the door and delivering meals to a family in the center section, I saw Scotty waving frantically from the kitchen. "Can you grab the delivery at the side door? I've already signed for it, but I can't leave the grill long enough to bring it in."

"On it."

I went to the side door beside the store room opposite the kitchen. As I poked my head outside, I could see the delivery truck already pulling into traffic again. Three huge boxes were stacked neatly on the pavement.

Wedging the door open with a piece of wood we kept on the floor just for that purpose, I managed to lift the first box and maneuver it into the store room. That one must have been the paper towels.

The second box was heavier. Seriously heavier. But I couldn't very well leave it outside to be stolen. Twisting it slightly, I tried to visualize lifting it before I actually did. I'd have to lift my chin, and hold it close to my body so it was more controlled.

But I'd have to hurry, since I could hear some sort of truck or van parking in the lot just behind me.

Swiveling the box a little more so that I could get a better grip, I lifted carefully with my legs, leaning back slightly. I had no idea what was inside, but if it was this heavy, it was probably breakable.

Three steps to the door, I was already out of breath. I managed to lean it against the door frame with my knee wedged under it. Although I wanted to set it down, I didn't know if I'd be able to pick it up again.

I shook out my arms, then lifted the box again. Turning slightly sideways to step inside, I wobbled as the box lurched to the left and started to fall as I scrambled to hold on with a shriek.

"Steady," a deep voice rumbled directly in my ear. I heard a thump as a hand landed under the box, and another hand grabbed my hip so that I didn't crash to the ground myself.

I started, my entire body pressed against the stranger's. Then I turned to find myself staring up into deep green eyes.

"I've got it, little lady," he grinned. "Just tell me where I'm going."

I stepped away to give him room to follow me down the hall, trying not to stare at the gorgeous man who had just rescued me. He was even bigger than my construction buddies. Instantly my hands began to fiddle with my apron and I couldn't stop biting my lip.

It took me a few seconds to find my voice. "If you could put it in the store room, that would be great. Thanks so much." I opened the door for him, and he placed the box down gently, as if the weight meant nothing to him.

"Hold on, I'll grab the other one."

He darted back out to grab the third box, kicking out the piece of wood so that the door closed behind him. After the last box was in the store room, he smiled down at me.

"I'm sorry I grabbed you, but you were about to fall off the step."

"That's okay. Thank you."

He turned toward the kitchen and took a sniff. "Damn. I guess I'm having the burger. Is it all right if I go out this way?" He pointed towards the front of the diner.

"Sure. Thank you."

"You're welcome." He paused, giving me a smile that

nearly knocked me over. We were very close together in the narrow hallway, and it was hard to believe how much I wanted to step closer instead of away. He smelled incredible, but it was his energy that really drew me in.

I watched as he went out to sit with Taylor and Bob, still feeling the warmth of his hand on my hip, and remembering the blaze of those unbelievable eyes when they locked on mine. *So this is their boss*, I thought. *Oh, my.*

I'd never been so close to a man who was so beautiful. Tingles ran up and down my arms as if I'd just met a rock star or something. The desire to have him hold me again was wild.

Yet somehow I had to pull myself together and channel my "Claudia the waitress" personality again. I was here to make a living, not lust after a man who was obviously way out of my league.

**2**

———

**VAUGHAN**

When I sat down beside Bob and reached for the water in front of me, I noticed my hand was actually shaking slightly. For the first time ever, I'd almost lost my cool in front of a woman.

"You made it," Taylor said with his slightly too-loud laugh.

"Yeah, finally got that last supply order in," I said, glancing around the diner.

It was quaint in all of the best ways. Plus, looking around at the vinyl booths, the checkered floor tiles, and the old-fashioned soda counter gave me a great excuse to actually check out the breathtaking waitress properly.

There was something in those soft blue eyes that softened my heart and stiffened the rest of me at the same time. Something that made me need to throw my arms around her and never let go. Even touching her hip to steady her had made me feel masculine in a way I'd never experienced before.

Either I was losing my mind, dehydrated from working

outside all day, or I was falling for this beautiful girl already. Was that even possible?

"I found this place a couple of weeks ago," Bob said. "Trust me, you're going to love the burger."

"They even have those sweet potato fries you like," Taylor said.

As the server walked toward us, I noticed a slightly worried look. Then she seemed to transform her energy with a giant, sassy smile. "Great," she said, with a hand on her hip. "Now I'm supposed to keep an eye on *three* of you?"

"Don't worry," Taylor said. "Vaughan is the boss, so he's relatively well behaved."

She was no longer the timid, off-balance girl from the doorway. It was like she had pulled a new personality on over her head like a comfortable sweater. I had to admit, I was intrigued with both versions.

Holding out my hand, I said, "Vaughan. The boss. And you are?"

Her beautiful lips pursed for a second, then she shook my hand. "Claudia. Fetcher of burgers, pourer of coffee, and wrangler of rowdy construction workers, apparently."

Bob and Taylor laughed. I released her hand, but darted my fingertips forward to brush against her inner wrist. Her eyes sparkled as she smiled.

"Let's get down to brass tacks," she said, pulling a little notepad from her skirt. "You're all having coffee, right?"

We nodded, then she continued. "Bob is having a double cheeseburger with fries, which comes with a small salad, and we're going to fight back and forth until he eventually eats it because it's just easier to do as I say and vegetables are good for you."

She shot him a pointed look, making him grin. He nodded, handing her back the menu.

"Taylor, last time you had the chicken sandwich, so I'm guessing today you're going to have the BLT with onion rings."

"Yes, Ma'am."

"Onions don't count as a vegetable when they're fried, so you're getting a side salad as well and that's final."

His bottom lip drooped in a dramatic pout, but he nodded.

"New guy," she said, tapping her pencil against the notepad. "You liked the smell of the burgers in the back hallway. But..." She looked me up and down carefully. The other guys were wearing slightly disheveled t-shirts, but I was in a black button down. Suddenly I was awfully glad I had scrubbed my face, combed my hair, and pulled on a fresh shirt before I left.

"You're into the classics, but with a twist," she said. "Double burger with sautéed onions, Dijon mustard, a tiny whiff of barbecue sauce...with sweet potato fries." Her head cocked to the side. "Am I close?"

"Spot on."

I handed back the menu, and she started to turn away, then took a step back and stared at me again. "And you really want a thick slab of marble cheese on that burger, but you were too polite to say that I missed it."

A deep chuckle rumbled up from my belly. It came out much louder than I intended, and actually took hold of me, making me helpless for a solid ten seconds. "You're absolutely right."

Her ponytail whipped through the air as she spun away again, leaving me with my mouth hanging open.

"Oh shit," Taylor whispered loudly. "Bob, I think we have a problem."

"What's that?"

"Boss man is smitten."

"Yeah, I noticed."

"Do you think we should warn her?" Taylor asked.

"No," Bob half-whispered back. "I think we should warn him. She's a really nice girl, and Vaughan wouldn't know what to do with her."

I chuckled again. "You know I can fire the both of you before she gets back here with the coffee pot, right?" Claudia was heading back toward us, and I glared at both of them. "Be cool or else."

Claudia served the coffee with another saucy smile directed right at me, then left to race laps around the diner.

As the guys talked about our latest construction project being right across the street from a gym with very sexy ladies in the window, I was only half listening. It was impossible to tear my eyes from Claudia. The way she was so patient and attentive with the elderly people. The way she played peekaboo with a menu to make a toddler laugh. The way she seemed to be constantly joking with the cook.

She was so gorgeous it was almost difficult to take her all in. Yet it was her fantastic spark of energy that made it impossible to tear my eyes away.

"Boss, your phone is beeping," Taylor said, pulling me out of my daze and back to reality.

"Sorry. Thanks."

It was a long, wordy text from my assistant Cheryl, warning me that my ex-girlfriend Jessica would be coming to the event celebrating the opening of the new hospital wing this Saturday night. Her date was a doctor there.

Instantly my fabulous mood turned dark. We had busted our asses to get that hospital contract, and pulled in every favor to make sure the job was perfect, and completed exactly on time. Apparently we were the only construction company to ever hit a deadline for them right on the nose. The big summer bash to celebrate the opening of the wing before all of the furniture got moved in was supposed to be the party of the year.

Now I was supposed to go stag while Jessica showed up with a doctor?

Dammit.

Jessica and I had only dated for about two months, and we had broken up over a year and a half ago. Yet that conniving little...*person*...still got under my skin.

She was a social climber of the worst kind. I found out that she had been using my private files to get the contact info of the owners of the corporations I was building for.

Since then, she had been like a termite, trying to worm her way in to grab more information. Phone calls to the office, pretending that we were still together. Calls and texts to me, my assistant, and others. It was bordering on harassment. She would just show up places, expecting to be let in so that she could meet people that she could later use in her bizarre quest to connect with all of the city's wealthiest people.

It was very distracting, at a time when I was very busy trying to expand the company now that I'd taken over from Dad completely.

I glanced up to see Bob looking at me strangely. "I know that look," he said. "What has Jessica done now?"

"Nothing. Just a heads up from Cheryl that she's going to be there on Saturday with some doctor as her date."

"You need to one up her," Bob said. "Show up with someone even more amazing."

"Those things are lousy for a real date," I said, shaking my head. "It's a networking thing. I'd never bring a woman I was interested in to one of those. She'd be bored to tears."

Taylor's eyes were blazing. I'd always suspected that he had more dirt on Jessica than he let on, since he seemed even more angry with her than I was. I knew that he had to escort her out of dangerous construction zones more than once.

"You need to stick it to that nasty piece of work," Taylor said. "Get yourself a gorgeous girl, and show up looking so happy that it makes Jessica cry."

"Not just a date," Bob said, drumming his fingers thoughtfully on the formica table top. "Make her pretend to be your fiancée or something. You know, like, serious. Make sure Jessica knows she never has another chance with you, ever."

"Trust me, she'd never want me," I said, forcing a smile. "She's looking for a guy who is super successful and mega rich. I was just a stepping stone."

Bob frowned as he reached out to clap the back of my shoulder. "I'm sorry, boss. I know. And all the more reason that I think you should take this opportunity to stick it to her once and for all."

Taylor laughed far too loudly at the double entendre. I didn't bother to tell him that I had never quite "stuck it" to Jessica at all. We had rarely been alone, since she had dragged me out to event after event, then said she was exhausted at the end of every night.

I couldn't help feeling that I dodged a bullet there. She was so determined to be a trophy wife I could see her getting knocked up on purpose.

"You need to show up with a girl who has things that Jessica never will," Bob said, grinning widely.

I looked up to see Claudia's radiant smile as she came toward us with three huge plates.

"Claudia would be perfect!" Taylor boomed. "She's ten

times prettier, and so sweet that she would make that evil witch sick."

Claudia set the plates in front of each of us. "You want me to make someone sick?" she giggled. "Honey, that is the opposite of what I do. I spread joy and great food."

"Claudia, do you have plans for Saturday night?" Bob asked.

I elbowed him hard in the ribs. "Shut your mouth."

"Come on, boss, you know she'd be perfect," he said.

Claudia stood there expectantly with her hands on her hips, her little sneaker tapping. "I've got orders, boys. Spit it out."

"Don't—" I started, but Taylor was quick and loud, as always.

"Vaughan's ex-girlfriend is showing up at an event this Saturday night that is supposed to be to celebrate an incredible project that his company built. It would be awesome if he could show her up by arriving with a gorgeous fiancée on his arm."

Claudia looked at each of us in turn, then rolled her eyes. "What – I'm not good enough to be a full-fledged wife? Don't waste my time, boys."

She waved to the plates in front of us. "I'm not even having this discussion until you tell me what compliments I'm to send back to Scotty."

She dashed away, returning with ketchup, barbecue sauce, and vinegar. "I suggest a half ketchup half barbecue sauce mix for those fries," she said to Taylor.

"If we eat everything on our plates like good little boys, will you consider being Vaughan's date?" Taylor asked.

"Oh, I don't think I'd ever go out with a man who didn't have the nerve to ask me himself," she said with a cheeky grin.

Then her eyes flashed to mine, and I saw something magical. She wanted me to ask her. I could see hope, mixed with nervousness, as if she wasn't sure whether she should let her sassy waitress mask slip.

This was my moment. I could either let the idea fade and brush the whole thing off as a joke, or I could take this opportunity to ask Claudia out. Even if we didn't go to Saturday's event, I really did want to show her that I thought she was the most incredible woman I'd ever met.

I stood up and went over to the end of the counter where there was a small vase of plastic flowers. Pulling them out, I turned to her and fell to one knee.

A couple of white haired ladies at the front gasped, but I figured this would give them a fun story to tell.

"Claudia, I know we just met, but would you please be my wife just for this Saturday night?"

My heart was pounding along to the old fifties love song playing quietly in the background. I waited while Claudia's expression morphed from disbelief to amusement. "What do I wear to such a thing?" she whispered.

"I'll buy you whatever you want."

Her hands twisted in her apron. "Um, we'll need some... backstory and stuff if we're going to pretend to be married."

"We'll have coffee this week and get our story straight. It can be whatever you want. Please?"

She hesitated, while one of the ladies in the front called out, "Just say yes, honey. My coffee's gettin' cold."

"Yes," she finally said, taking the flowers from me.

Bob and Taylor cheered as I stood up. I wanted to hug her, but she looked so nervous that I didn't dare.

Then she smiled brightly. "Now eat your dinner and let me work," she laughed. "Gosh, I knew that more than two of you would be a handful."

As I walked by her, my hand brushed her upper arm in a tiny caress. The way she smiled up at me made my heart beat with a strange new jazzy rhythm that I'd never felt before.

I already knew that this date wasn't going to be fake. Sure, the part about being married was, but we already clearly liked each other.

It was sudden, but I already knew that we belonged together, and this was going to become so much more.

# 3

## CLAUDIA

For the ten thousandth time, I couldn't believe I was doing this. Spinning in front of the mirror in a floor-length silk gown, I had to admit that the soft silvery blue brought out my eyes and made my skin glow.

"It fits you like a dream," my new sales lady Jeanette said excitedly. "Let's try it with the shoes."

Although I had begged her for the lowest heels possible, it seemed that two and a half inches was as reasonable as she was willing to go. I hitched up the skirt so that she could slip them on for me in a way that made me feel like Cinderella. They were a very slightly darker silver, and once I dropped the skirt, the toes barely peeped out from under the hem.

"Let's see you walk," Jeanette said. Her enthusiasm was contagious.

I was relieved that Vaughan had insisted that he would take care of absolutely all the logistics for our date. Over text this morning, I told him that this was my day off. He had immediately arranged for me to get a dress and shoes this afternoon, and then I was meeting him for coffee later.

Walking slowly past the enormous mirrors, I had to admit that the dress was incredibly flattering. It showed just enough cleavage for a cocktail party, and nipped in at the waist, flaring at the hips to give me more of an hourglass figure than I would ever have thought possible.

"Chin up," Jeanette commanded. "Small, even steps. This is a dress where you have to walk like a princess."

Since I assumed that princesses normally didn't cuss, I kept my internal comments to myself.

I managed to walk relatively smoothly across the room, then returned to her with only a slight wobble in the new heels.

"The thing about heels is you can use them as an excuse to hold onto your man as much as you like," Jeanette grinned. "You'll have to wear them around the house for a half hour here and there before your event, though, to break them in."

She turned me around one more time. "I really think this outfit is the one. What about you?"

Since I didn't know anything about fashion other than what itched and what didn't, I was going to have to take her word for it. But it was certainly flattering, and pretty simple. Anything fussy or over the top always looked tacky to me.

"Yes, if you're sure this is what other people will be wearing. It's not too much?"

Jeanette smiled. "Before you got here I double checked with my friend who is an event planner. She says that hospital openings run the gamut from work outfits, to cocktail dresses, to extremely formal, like black tie formal. What we have here I would consider eighty-five percent formal. Not over the top, but you'll definitely be one of the best dressed women in the room."

"Okay. That sounds reasonable."

"Do you have someone to do your hair and make up?"

I spun toward her, and luckily she grabbed my elbow so that I didn't fall. "No. Is that normal? I thought I should just...wear a bit more eyeliner."

Jeanette smiled kindly, leading me over to a velvet seat so I could slip the shoes off.

"Mr. Walsh was adamant that I help you get absolutely everything you need," she said. "Don't worry – you change out of that and I'll find you someone who is available Saturday evening to doll you up."

"Thank you."

By the time I came out of the change room, she had a business card in hand. "Lauren just had a cancellation, so I snapped her up immediately. She's great. I told her about the event, and she already has a plan."

"Thank you. I really appreciate this."

She added her own business card and slipped them both into the outside pocket of my purse. "If you stick with this amazing man, I have a feeling you're going to want to visit me again."

"Absolutely," I said with a smile, even though I had no idea whether Vaughan and I would be going on more than one date.

I still didn't know quite what to think about the whole thing. Vaughan was gorgeous, but it was much more than that. I loved the way he joked around with his coworkers. I loved the way he took his time to actually taste his food. And even though he had only touched me twice, in very innocent ways, there was something about the electrifying prickle of his hand on me that made me need more.

But was it possible to be addicted so instantly? It was bizarre. Yet it was definitely something I wanted to explore further.

Apparently Vaughan had left his credit card number with the store, so Jeanette boxed and bagged everything up for me.

"Just one more thing," she said, leading me over to the end of the counter where she had arranged three ties that almost perfectly matched my dress. "You can either pick the one that you think matches the dress best, the one that you like best, or the one that you think he would like the best," she laughed.

Two of them were patterned, and a bit distracting. The third was simpler and matched the dress perfectly, with very faint vertical pinstripe lines in a lighter silver.

"That one," I said, pointing.

"Perfect."

As I left the store, Vaughan rushed up to grab the bags from me. "What are you doing here?" I asked in surprise.

"I couldn't wait to see you," he said with a grin. "Plus, I didn't think that my wife should be hauling packages around." He looked up and down the street. "Where did you park?"

"I don't have a car," I laughed. "I took the bus."

His eyes widened in horror. "Claudia, I'm so sorry. I didn't think. I should have sent you a car."

"It's fine. I'm used to the bus."

I followed him to a huge work truck that said Walsh Construction across the side. "So you own the business?"

"Yes." He opened the passenger door, carefully set my packages inside, then reached for my hand. As he helped me up the big step, I was struck again by how ridiculously large he was. But it wasn't scary. It was comforting, somehow. I also noticed that he kept my hand in his for as long as possible, which was charming.

Once I was buckled in, he ran around to the other side.

"Yeah, my grandfather started the company, dad took it over and made it grow, and now I guess it's my turn." He began to drive south.

"Where are we going?" I asked.

"I get the impression that you've been working too hard this summer. So consider this an evening's worth of vacation time," he smiled. "I'm taking you to the beach."

It was as if Vaughan had somehow read my mind, or taken one look at me and known exactly what I needed. After working on my classes during the day, and my shifts at night, as well as not having any friends in town, my summer activities list had been short verging on zero.

"Trust me," Vaughan said with a smile as we pulled into traffic. "I know the perfect place."

We pointed out stores and restaurants we liked on the drive, and I appreciated the variety of his interests. I was glad that a bookshop was among his favorite stores. Tough and smart was definitely a good combination.

We arrived at an incredible restaurant down by the water, very close to the sand. It was breezy and comfortable, while still being quite elegant. We were led to the second floor, to a balcony patio that overlooked the waves.

"How's this?" Vaughan asked, as he pulled out my chair.

"Perfect, thank you."

I loved that he pulled out the chair beside me to sit in, not the one across the table.

As he sat down, I used the opportunity to take a closer look at his broad, hard body. He might be the boss of his company, but he certainly did some of the work himself. Those thick arms definitely came from hauling lumber, not fancy gym workouts.

Although his dark blue button down shirt looked fresh as if he had just changed it, he still managed to look a bit rough around the edges. The deep tan, the faint but charming smile lines around his eyes, and the casual way he held himself made me like him even more.

I hadn't felt an attraction to anyone in so long. There hadn't been time, or I'd made other excuses. But here was a nice, handsome man who was apparently interested in me. There was just no way to tell whether it was genuine attraction on his part, or whether I was simply fixing his ex-girlfriend problem.

If nothing else, though, this was a perfect opportunity to see if I could maintain my new outgoing personality when I wasn't working at the diner. If Vaughan needed a wife to impress people, I was going to have to speak with strangers, and be bubbly.

I was going to have to appear absolutely delighted with everything. In other words, I was going to have to fake a lot of sincerity. Sure. No problem.

The server brought over menus, and although Vaughan ordered a beer, he suggested I have one of their fancy fruity drinks. "I suppose you're not having one because they're not manly enough?" I teased.

He looked sheepish. "Actually, that's not it. Sugary drinks always make the booze hit me harder, and I'm driving you around. With just one beer, I know that I'm good."

His honesty was refreshing, as was his ability to admit limitations. So far, Vaughan was checking every box in what I wanted in a fake husband.

I decided on a raspberry apple rum slushy, then we chose several appetizers so that we could share everything.

"I haven't been here in years," Vaughan said with a smile that showcased his perfect teeth. "Mom and Dad used to bring me here once or twice every summer."

"Why don't the three of you come anymore?" I asked.

"Mom always had her heart set on living on the beach in Florida, so they retired there a year and a half ago."

"Oh. Well, that's nice too, I guess."

Vaughan's hand reached to cover mine on the table. "I really appreciate you coming to this event, Claudia. I hope you realize that I'd been trying to figure out a way to ask you out before the guys piped up."

I snickered. "But you wanted to make sure that the burger was fabulous first, right?"

He chuckled, shaking his head. "I just didn't want to be one of those guys who tries to pick up the server. I know It must happen to you twenty times a night."

I shook my head. "Nope. Not even close."

"Good," he grinned. "That means not many single men come into your work. That makes me feel a lot better."

Was he a tiny bit jealous already? Possessive? I don't know why, but that made my stomach flutter.

"So," I said, retracting my hand to nervously tuck my hair behind my ears. "How do you want to play this fake marriage thing?"

His eyes sparkled. "As much as we can base in truth, the better. How long have you worked at the diner?"

"It's always been part time, but just over a year."

"Perfect. I met you there about a year ago, and six months ago finally asked you out. We dated for two months, then got engaged, and were married a month later. How does that sound?"

My eyebrow raised as I looked at him. "That's awfully quick, mister. Am I that kind of girl?"

"We couldn't help ourselves," he said, as his fingertips tucked my hair behind my ear again for good measure, smiling. "I wanted you to move in with me because I wanted to see you all day, every day. You didn't want to move in without a commitment. So I surprised you with a ring, and you surprised me with the perfect wedding idea."

"Perfect," I said. "Super romantic without being ludicrously over the top."

Vaughan's amused smile suddenly dropped. "A few coworkers and clients have been to my house. Jessica has, too. Are you free Friday night?"

Good grief. I finally get asked out for a Friday night date, and it's to do reconnaissance for a semi-fake date mission.

"We close at ten on Fridays."

"Will you come to my house, and look around?" he asked. "We can make up some stories of how you've tried to change me by fixing my terrible taste in lamps."

I realized with delight that I'd never once had to force laughter with him. Normally with customers, and other strangers, I tried to laugh a lot to cover my nerves. With Vaughan, I was almost totally myself.

"Sure. How many houseplants do you have?"

He hung his head in shame, causing his hair to flop across his forehead. "None."

"Well, you have until Friday to add at least five: for the kitchen, dining room, and living room."

"Yes, dear."

Even though he was teasing, I loved how sweet he was.

Our food arrived, and as we ate we tried to figure out how many favorite TV shows, movies, and bands we had in common. The number surprised us both. We had very similar taste in both police dramas and bizarre British comedies. I loved that he enjoyed documentaries as much as I did, and that he went out to see indie bands now and then.

"What are you taking at school?" he asked, as he munched on a skewer of barbecued fruit.

"Public Relations."

"Cool. How much longer do you have to go?"

"I actually only have a few projects left, then I'm finished in two weeks. In October I have a job lined up with Presence Publicity, on the other side of town. I've been freelancing for them already, writing copy for websites, other little stuff like that."

Vaughan reached his hand out to squeeze mine. "That's amazing. I'm so proud of you."

I could tell that he really meant it, which was surprisingly touching. "It's nothing compared to running a construction empire," I laughed.

He gave me a sheepish smile. "I didn't build the empire. I simply took it over and now I'm doing my best to grow it even more than my dad did. I'm fully aware of how privileged I am to have a great business just handed to me."

"But do you really enjoy it?" I asked. "If you were to start all over again from scratch, would this be your dream?"

"Absolutely." He held my gaze as he fed me a braised raspberry, and my stomach fluttered. "I've been building things since I was able to hold blocks. Creating and constructing is in my blood."

"I like that it's your choice."

"Well, it was that or do crochet like my mom," he chuckled. Holding up his hand, we surveyed his thick fingers. "Do I look suited to yarn and those little hook thingies?"

I laughed with him, but realized I was getting more and more overheated. All I could think of was how much I wanted his hands on me. He was so confident, so huge, that I couldn't help wondering what things would be like if we were somewhere private, and he was using those thick fingers...

*Oh my.*

I finished the last melted bits of my sugary drink while

Vaughan paid the bill. He took my arm as we walked toward the beach.

"Even though you only have a few weeks left, I want to make sure you get a summer," he said.

"Hey, I have plenty of summer. It's when Scotty begs me to bring him ice water, and my hair falls flat every time I step into the kitchen."

Vaughan attempted to scowl, but it morphed into a grin. "Oh, come on. You need some sand in your shoes and some sunshine on your skin."

He pulled me over to a notice board. "Let's see if they have any summer concerts coming up on the beach."

My eyes skimmed over the ads for guitar lessons, a notice for a Thursday night beach drum circle, and a few lost and found posters.

We circled to the other side, which held larger posters. "Here we are," Vaughan said, pointing to a large green sheet. "Do you like jazz? That would be a fun night out."

"Sure," I muttered, trying to smile.

My eyes had locked onto a bright poster reminding people of the upcoming election for Mayor. Pierce Lorimer was running again, even though he had lost last time.

That drunk, conniving bastard kept trying to dig his hooks into this area so that he could do favors for his friends. He'd been working towards getting elected as Mayor for years. By some accounts, he had a good shot of winning this year, which made my blood run cold.

"Hey, isn't that your last name?" Vaughan said, pointing to where I was staring uncomfortably at the poster. "Any relation?"

"Jazz would be great," I cut him off with a grin, pointing just under it and changing the subject. "And there's also an old time dance band next week."

Vaughan wrapped his arm around my waist, dancing me around in a circle. "I'm not a very good dancer, but it's easy enough to shuffle around on sand, right?"

The way he held me filled me with longing. He was so sweet. I knew that I shouldn't get my hopes up, for fear that my heart might get broken, yet it was already out of my hands. That ship had definitely sailed.

My head fell to rest on Vaughan's shoulder as we slowly circled again, ignoring the people all around us. Snuggling against him felt perfect.

I wanted him. I needed him to want me as more than a temporary convenient relationship. Just once, I would love to feel like I truly belonged with someone, somewhere. To feel that I was good enough for a good person.

# 4

## VAUGHAN

Things seemed to be working out absolutely perfectly so far with Claudia, as smoothly if we were following blueprints. Although this was definitely the most unconventional way I'd ever started dating a woman, the forced closeness of having to get to know each other quickly actually seemed helpful.

The more I got to know Claudia, the more I knew that she was absolutely the one. From the way she took such tentative first bites to be sure her food wasn't too hot, to the way she paused to think before she spoke, everything about her was enchanting. I loved that she was thoughtful, and seemed mature for her age, while at the same time being so fresh and vibrant.

Holding her in my arms and dancing around was both silly and a great way to tell that she enjoyed my touch. Yet I didn't want to overwhelm her too soon. Reluctantly letting her go, I took her hand so that we could walk across the rocks and down to the sand.

The poster for the upcoming Mayoral election reminded me of something important.

"Claudia, there are going to be a lot of politicians and prominent business people at the event on Saturday."

I had no idea why she instantly looked so nervous.

"Most of them are pretty boring, and we don't necessarily have to talk to them very much," I continued, "but a lot of them think I'm some sort of young upstart because I haven't been in the business for fifty years, and I'd like to change that opinion."

Her eyebrow raised as she looked at me. "I don't think you're anywhere near fifty, are you?"

"I'm thirty-eight. But even though I've been working for my dad and learning about the business since I was sixteen, I've only been in charge of the company for a short time. Also, some of these guys have known me since I was much younger. Once they see me with a beautiful wife on my arm, it might reinforce the fact that I'm actually all grown up and the one in charge."

"I see what you mean," she said. "So as well as shutting up Jessica once and for all, this could be good for your business?"

"Exactly. It's an accidental bonus, but I wanted to be up front about it."

Her beautiful blue eyes blazed up at me. "Anything in particular I should say to them?"

"No, just be your charming self. Plus the usual small talk about how brilliant the hospital wing is, and how it's the best construction job you've ever seen in your entire life."

"Oh, of course," she said quickly. "I haven't even seen it, yet it's the sturdiest thing ever built. I'm sure of it."

We laughed together, walking along the edge of the water. The sun was just beginning to set, sending warm ripples of light through her dark hair. As cute as she was in a ponytail at work, her hair looked stunning flowing loosely around her shoulders.

I stopped to pull her against me. "I know this is a strange first date, Claudia. Saturday is going to be even odder. But I really like you, and when this is over, I hope that we can go out on a ton of regular dates, and just hang out."

"Just without the fake wife part," she said. "Yeah, I'd like that too."

My hand slid around her waist as her lips tipped up to mine so perfectly, so naturally that I had no doubt that we were thinking the exact same thing.

The gentle kiss was slow and soft. Full of promise and possibility. When she didn't pull away, my arm tightened around her, tasting those beautiful lips as the kiss deepened. Her hand slipped around my neck, our hips pressing together, everything happening so smoothly that it felt like a perfect dream.

When Claudia pulled away, she looked up at me with a shy smile. It was as if she wanted to say something, but we were both speechless.

"Excuse me."

We turned to see a young man in baggy shorts and sandals with a rather large, expensive looking camera. "Hey, sorry to interrupt. But I couldn't resist taking a couple of pictures of you guys just now. With the sunset behind you it was just incredible. Look."

He came closer to show us the view screen. Claudia and I were almost in silhouette against the vivid pink and orange sunset, our very first kiss captured just as the waves missed our feet by inches.

"I can send this to you if you like," he said.

Digging in my pocket, I pulled out my wallet to hand him my business card and two fifties. "May I officially hire you for a super quick photo shoot right now? And can you send me the highlights tomorrow?"

"Sure, thanks!" he said, as his eyes lit up.

Claudia's grin was so beautiful that I felt it as much as I saw it. "Great idea. You'll post a few of these online over the next few days, right?"

"Yes. And it can't hurt to have them on hand." I leaned down to whisper in her ear, "Plus you're so beautiful I'm going to miss you every time we're apart." I adored the way her eyes blazed at that.

The photographer introduced himself as Evan and we got to work. Over the next five to ten minutes, he directed us in a variety of classic couples poses.

I tossed Claudia in the air with her hair flying. Carrying her to the edge of the water, I pretended to nearly drop her in. She sat on the stone wall at the edge of the sand so that I had to look up at her, holding her hand.

As we flipped through the shots, there were a few that looked like they were taken in an entirely different place.

"How hard would it be to lighten my shirt and make her dress green or something in this one?" I said, pointing. "So that it looks like it was taken on a different day."

Evan took a closer look. "Oh yeah – no problem. That'll take a few minutes, tops."

We shook his hand then began to walk slowly back to my truck.

"I wasn't expecting a photo shoot," Claudia said.

"Sometimes things just work out," I said. "Imagine if it had taken me a few days to ask you out. Taylor might have beaten me to it."

Her tinkling laugh was so sweet.

"Sugary slush drink, roasted fruit, sunset on the beach,

and an impromptu photo shoot. I think we packed a lot of summer into the day for you," I said.

"Not to mention that over-the-top shopping trip. Thank you for that. I've never been anywhere so ridiculously posh."

I wanted to tell her that was just the beginning. That I wanted to spoil her and treasure her for a very long time. Yet it seemed too soon. I didn't want to burden her with plans for the future at the end of our very first evening together.

Just before I helped her into the truck, I pointed to a new condo tower under construction down the beach. "That's one of our projects."

"Wow," she said, looking around. "That place is going to have an incredible view."

"That's the idea. It's going to be the tallest building in the area for a very long time."

On the drive home we chatted about our favorite websites, how we liked to decompress after a hard day of work, and important comfort foods. Once again, we had so much in common.

The bright, animated way she spoke revealed a softer side than the one she showed at the diner. As if she were letting down her walls and allowing me to see her true self.

Every single version of Claudia that I'd seen so far made me excited to see more. This beautiful, thoughtful girl already had my heart more than any other woman had before in the space of twenty-four hours.

I couldn't imagine how smitten I would be once I saw her all glammed up at the opening.

# 5

# CLAUDIA

After that completely magical date, it was hard to go back to the real world. But I needed to stay ahead of my work. On Wednesday I finished writing a paper so that I could proofread it on Thursday, and got caught up with some of my freelance work.

All the while, Vaughan and I were continually texting each other tiny details of our days.

He sent me a photo of the sunrise from that beach condo tower. I sent him a photo of the steam coming off my morning coffee. We went through our do lists for the day, awarding each other stars for getting everything done.

I loved that such a big, rough guy was so sensitive and playful. Vaughan was honest, too: he didn't try to edit his life to just show me the best parts. He was open about being hooked on construction disaster shows so that he could both learn and gloat. He confessed that once a month he allowed himself to eat a whole pizza on his own while watching action movies. His version of self-care was remarkably relatable.

I also loved the photos he sent to me of us on the

beach. I couldn't resist making the silhouette shot my laptop background, since it filled me with joy every time I saw it.

Thursday I was able to turn in my paper just before leaving for work, and by the time Taylor and Bob rolled in, my smile wasn't artificial at all.

"Hey, Claudia," Taylor said as he lounged back in the booth. "How's the new husband working out?"

Bob shot him a glare, then smiled at me, lowering his voice. "You two are going to be a hit on Saturday."

"Especially when Jessica's jaw hits the floor," Taylor laughed.

I handed them menus, knowing that they likely didn't need them at this point. "She can't be that bad," I said. "Who knows? We might even end up friends."

They shared a look. "Not likely," Bob said carefully. "There is a whole list of words we generally try not to use to describe women, and all of them completely apply to Jessica."

I had to hold my order pad over my mouth as I snorted a laugh.

"Look, Claudia," Taylor said, finally lowering his voice, "You're a nice girl. The sort of sweet woman that every man really does want. Jessica can never be that. So her attempt to show off and one-up Vaughan is going to fall flat. With luck this will do the trick and she'll finally stop trying to make him look unprofessional once and for all."

"Well, that does sound very annoying, so I'm happy to help," I said. "Now, I assume you're both having coffee?"

"Yes."

"Then by the time I get back here with the pot, you'll both know what you're having, and that will include salads, boys."

Taylor stuck his bottom lip out as Bob said, "Yes, Mrs. Walsh."

Giggling, I had to admit I preferred the sound of that to my own name. As I went to grab the coffee pot, Scotty was just setting a tuna melt on the pass. "Customers just love it when you boss them around. How do you do that?"

"I took a couple of acting classes in high school," I whispered. "There's a certain tone that people don't mess with. They want to play along. Plus I watch their eyes to be sure that they're really laughing with me."

He chuckled, hustling back to the grill while whistling.

The evening passed quickly, and I realized that time seemed to flow differently now that I was always connected to someone. Vaughan and I had a constant link of text conversation that made everything go faster. Before I knew it, it was Friday night and he was picking me up from work.

He waited until he was helping me into the truck to give me a tiny kiss hello, then we drove to his house. It was stunning – a large classic red brick home on a rather huge plot of land.

"This is all yours?"

"Yup," he said, helping me down from the truck. I loved the way he used any excuse to put his hands on me. It was adorably saucy. "It's similar to my parents' house, but I wanted something a bit smaller."

If this was his idea of small, I couldn't imagine what their house was like.

Vaughan walked me in through the front door, and I stared around at the foyer and main room. Kicking off my shoes, I dropped my purse and walked through to the living room.

Then I burst out laughing. There was a hanging plant in the windows of the living room, dining room, and kitchen.

Plus tall standing plants in several corners, and a row of flowering plants along the kitchen window. I quickly counted fifteen in all, then nearly doubled over in a fit of giggles.

"What?" he asked, patiently waiting for me to pull myself together.

"I meant to scatter at least five plants through the whole space," I sputtered. "You put five plants in each room."

He rolled his eyes, joining my laughter. "Okay, now I understand. The plant service did say it seemed a bit much for the dining room. There's also a fluffy green thing in the upstairs washroom."

Impulsively I threw my arms around him in a hug. "You're a very good husband, fulfilling my request to the letter."

He gave me a squeeze, then kissed the top of my head. "Anything my gorgeous and amazing wife desires, I'll do my best to provide it."

Even though we were joking, it was overwhelmingly sweet. "You hired a plant service?"

"Yeah," he said with a shrug of those wide shoulders. "I don't know what stuff needs what sort of light. I didn't want anything to have a lousy life because I don't know what I'm doing. They printed out sheets with watering instructions, and I'll have them come back every two months to check on everything and fertilize or whatever."

He was actually concerned with the lives of plants. Vaughan really was the most precious man I'd ever met.

He took me on a tour of the entire house, and all joking aside I honestly did question his taste when it came to a few of the lamps. It didn't take long for me to get a feel for his style. I couldn't help thinking of the small changes that I'd make if I were to move in someday.

I knew that I was thinking way too far ahead, but I couldn't help it. Everything was going so well so far.

"Here, let me show you the backyard," Vaughan said, keeping an arm around me as we went out the sliding kitchen door.

Four old-fashioned lamp posts cast a faint glow. There was a massive barbecue grill, with sturdy wrought iron patio furniture.

"Motion sensors," he said, leading me to a bench out in the garden. There were more trees and shrubs than flowers, and I couldn't help thinking that a woman's touch throughout the entire space would bring everything together, give it that little extra oomph.

For the first time in my entire life, I could honestly imagine settling down with a man. Living our entire lives together. Working and cooking and lounging and...I knew it was way too soon to be thinking along those lines, but, again, I couldn't help it.

Everything was falling into place so smoothly and it was so easy to picture our entire future laid out before us. That thought made me as giddy as the warmth of Vaughan's hand skimming up and down my back as we sat close together.

"I like your house," I said softly.

"Our house," he gently corrected me.

"Right. Our house. I've been living here several months, I added the plants and I'm changing out a few of the lamps next weekend. Also, we're thinking about putting in an aquarium."

He turned us to face each other and quirked his right eyebrow up at me. "Oh, are we, now?"

"Yes. We both keep slightly strange hours during busy spells, so we're not quite settled enough for something furry. Don't worry – we're just thinking about it for now. It might be our Christmas present to each other over the holidays."

It felt so deeply perfect that we were both smiling as his lips met mine. His fingertips slipped into the back of my hair, as my hands gripped his thick biceps.

Vaughan lifted me, setting me on his lap. The indescribable hum pulling the two of us together was incredible. It felt like my body burned for his. As if we couldn't possibly be close enough.

My lips parted so that he could deepen the kiss as I clung to him. My breasts crushed against his chest, and I heard him groan.

Then I realized my thigh was brushing quite insistently against a very firm area in his jeans. It was intoxicating to think that he was so aroused just because of me. Just because of a little kiss.

How strange that it made me feel powerful, but it also told me that this oddly accelerated relationship was absolutely real. Well, mostly. Once we got through tomorrow night, things would probably be a bit more relaxed.

Trembling in his arms, I gasped softly as his tongue entered my mouth, exploring, tasting. When he finally pulled back to gaze into my eyes, I felt like I was floating.

"Claudia," he began, as his thumb ran down the side of my cheek. "My precious girl."

I reached up to tweak his nose with my finger. "Wife."

"Yes, dear," he said in that teasing singsong voice that I was falling in love with. Oh. Wow. I really was falling.

"We have a big day ahead tomorrow, gorgeous," he murmured softly against my ear until I shivered. "As much as I would love to take you upstairs, I think I should probably take you home so you can get a good night's rest."

"Yes, I guess so. I have to start getting ready at three."

Vaughan held me back another few inches so that he could stare at me. "Three? I'm not picking you up till six-forty-five."

"Yes. But I have to shower and do a scrub before the makeup artist arrives at four to do my face and hair."

He shook his head. "I'm so sorry."

"Really, it's okay. Actually, I've never gone anywhere so fancy before. It's going to be an adventure."

Vaughan's grin would have knocked me over if he wasn't holding me so tight. "Now that's an attitude I respect," he said. "Life is an adventure. New things are how we grow. I can't stand it when people have their minds made up about something when they haven't even tried it yet."

I knew that he was probably referring to Jessica, but certainly didn't want to think about her right now.

We walked out to the front foyer, and Vaughan grabbed his keys as I grabbed my purse. "Oh – I almost forgot." I took a long, flat cardboard box out of my bag and handed it to him.

"What's this?"

"Just look."

As he opened the lid his handsome face transformed into a smile of pure delight. "You got me a tie?"

"It matches my dress. Apparently, that's what couples do at shindigs like this."

"I love that it's simple," he said, running a finger over the silk. "Pinstripes are quite enough of a pattern for me." He looked up to see me grinning from ear to ear.

"Of course I'm going to know exactly what my husband wants," I said. "You're a no-nonsense guy. No paisley or houndstooth for you."

Vaughan set the box on a side table, gathering me into

his arms to dance around the foyer to whatever imaginary beat was in his head.

"I love that you already understand me," he murmured, as his strong hands caressed my back.

Feeling his body pressed to mine made my thighs quiver and my breath catch in my throat. It was heavenly. Terrifying. Exciting. Everything at once.

As I took brand new steps into the grand adventure of dating and having a boyfriend...sorry, make that a husband...I couldn't imagine trying to figure it out with anyone other than Vaughan.

6

———

## VAUGHAN

I knew that Saturday was going to be busy, but everything seemed to take twice as long as I had expected. Checking on one job site should have taken twenty minutes, but it stretched into an hour. Then there was a lineup at the bank and it took forever to grab something from a safety deposit box.

I actually had to stop for espresso on the way to pick up Claudia. Then I realized that I was a terrible husband for not knowing how she took her coffee, so I sent her a quick text.

**Me:** I'm doing a coffee run on the way to collect you. What would you like? Espresso? Latte?

Luckily she responded almost immediately.

**Claudia:** Americano with a pinch of cinnamon. You know – like we had on our honeymoon when we cruised by Italy. I can't believe you don't remember! :)

**Me:** Of course. How silly of me to forget.

**Me:** I'll be there in a few minutes.

**Claudia:** I'm almost ready.

By the time I got to her apartment, I was actually prickling with nerves. My company's marketing person had made a big deal about me finally bringing a date to one of these events. I tried to tell Yvonne that we didn't need any more media coverage, but I wasn't sure that she listened.

I was about to buzz Claudia's apartment number when she opened the door in front of me. "Were you waiting here in the lobby?" I asked.

"I just got downstairs," she said.

"You're supposed to let me come to you," I began to chuckle, then we stepped out in front of the building and I got a proper look at her.

My heart began to pound in a strange techno sort of rhythm that I'd never felt before.

Claudia was ravishing.

Her lovely dark hair was pinned up in some sort of fancy twist with a swirly silver clip. Somehow her eyes were even bigger, even bluer. She looked like a model. Or a doll. Or a photo of the perfect glamorous girl next door.

"What's wrong?" she asked breathlessly, fingers clenched around her tiny black purse that hung from a wrist strap.

"Absolutely nothing," I muttered.

My eyes raked over her cleavage, then paused at the curve of her hips. I needed to grab her. I needed to hold her against me immediately. I'd never had such a powerful reaction of raw desire before.

Blowing out a slow breath, I shook my head. "I just really can't believe how beautiful you are, Claudia. It's freaking me out, to be honest."

Her perfect rosy lips fell open, then she laughed out loud before pausing to look me up and down. "I have to say, you look very different in a suit."

"Good different or bad different?"

"Just different. I think I like both versions."

"Good."

Taking her arm, I led her to the car I'd hired for the night. There was no way I could get the seats in my work truck clean enough for fancy clothes. And I certainly didn't want to have to pass up any drinks if they were being offered by potential clients. More deals were made over whiskey than over coffee, Dad always said.

"Before we chug our coffee, I have to give you something," I said, pulling a little box from my pocket.

"Oh, right!" she said brightly. "You said you'd get a fake diamond ring."

"I never want to give you anything fake, Claudia. Even if it's just for one night."

She gasped as I opened the box, her hand fluttering up to hide her mouth. "That can't be real."

"It's my mother's ring," I said, taking Claudia's hand. Even though this was temporary, it felt like an important moment. "Claudia, will you be my wife for the night?"

"Yes," she whispered, her lovely eyes shining.

Slipping it on her fourth finger, it fit perfectly. "Dad got it for her on their fifth wedding anniversary. But once she had me a few years later, she gained a bit of weight, and she said it wasn't as comfortable anymore."

She stared down at the large square emerald that was flanked by two rectangular diamonds on either side. Then Claudia held it up beside my face. "It almost matches your eyes," she said softly. "Vaughan, I don't know if I should wear this."

"Yes, you absolutely should. I can't stand the thought of you wearing a cheap ring."

She bit her lip for a moment as she stared down at the sparkling gems, then looked up at me. "As long as you promise to be my bodyguard all night."

"Of course, dear."

I loved the way her eyes lit up whenever I used the slightest term of endearment with her. Every time I looked into Claudia's sweet eyes, I felt like I was seeing a new side of her. Getting to know her more and more.

Leaning forward, I pressed my lips to her gently, but she flinched backward. "Lipstick. Lauren said it's long wear, but I don't know how to fix it properly if it smudges."

"Then hold very still," I murmured. I ghosted my lips against hers with no pressure at all, just enough to make her breathing become erratic.

Then I slipped my hand up the back of her neck, taking hold of her without messing up her artfully arranged hair. Tilting her back, I kissed along her throat until she quivered in my arms. Her halting breath, and the way she twitched as I explored her soft skin, made me realize how desperately I wanted to take her right now.

Of course I wouldn't. It wasn't nearly time yet. But I couldn't help the passionate arousal that was crackling through me like flames.

Nipping at her ear, I kissed just below it, nuzzling her until she moaned softly. Then I kissed down her neck, slipping into the top of her dress to trace along the top of her breast.

Her fingers gripped the back of my hair as she held me against her. "Kiss me again," she gasped. "Please."

"Lipstick," I practically growled, holding her tightly in place as I barely brushed her lips with mine. Teasing us both so terribly was probably not a good idea before we had to walk into an event, but I couldn't resist.

Every gasp, every moan that escaped from those perfect lips made me feel like I was winning her over. Making her mine in dozens of microscopic ways.

Claudia's breath began to flutter in her throat as she tried to pull my mouth closer. I forced myself to release her, gently pushing us apart.

"Let's get to the coffee. We're going to need to stay perky all night long," I said.

Her cheeks were slightly flushed as her glassy eyes blinked quickly. "Good idea."

As we drank our coffee, I noticed that her eyes kept dropping to the ring. It was hard to tell if she was amused, touched, or whether everything was just a bit overwhelming.

I was surprised at how deeply wonderful it felt to put jewelry on this gorgeous girl. Everything was happening out of order with us, but hopefully it wouldn't matter once we got settled into this new relationship.

Claudia already drove me crazy in every possible way. She was sexy and sweet, light and charming. Nobody could possibly ask for more in a wife.

I already knew that once we spent a lot more time together and our lives became entwined, it wouldn't be long before I was giving her a ring that we picked out together, not something that I borrowed from my mother's safety deposit box.

# 7

## CLAUDIA

An hour into the event, my "Claudia the waitress" personality had been repurposed into my brand new "Claudia the sweet bubbly wife who is so proud of her new husband" personality, if admittedly a little less sassy.

I wasn't used to this much attention, but all of the other well-dressed couples seemed so eager to get to know us. I completely understood what Vaughan meant now. The couples were all gathered in a group, and single people weren't exactly shunned, but they were definitely on the fringes of the conversations.

Mayor Robert Bennett and his lovely wife Ellen were incredibly sweet to me, introducing me to everyone in the high-powered group. It was all the people who ran the city in the same room at once. It was a little intimidating, but it was also downright fascinating.

The entire time, Vaughan held my hand or kept his arm wrapped around me. It was impossible not to notice the way he glared at any man who let his eyes linger below my chin.

I'd never been treated like this before. As if I were someone truly special.

My body was still tingling from the explosive makeout session in the car. The heat we had together felt almost dangerous. Plus, being that intimate in semi-public was definitely a naughty thrill.

As much as Vaughan had shown me his physical desire for me in the car, now he was showing me how much he was emotionally invested in this budding relationship as well.

I loved how he was careful to make sure I got a few bites of food every twenty minutes when the servers circled by, and how he always made sure I had a fresh glass of champagne, while at the same time reminding me to take tiny sips and not drink it too quickly.

That was easy to remember, since I was already drunk on his affection. The way his fingertips meandered along my shoulder and arm. The way his fingers grasped mine. The way he slipped his thumb down the back of my neck, then down my spine, making me shiver.

At first, I had been nervous that this dress was cut quite low at the back, but it kept Vaughan touching me at all times.

Jeanette's advice had been absolutely on point. I was dressed perfectly. Definitely in the top ten percent of the hundred or so women wandering through the lobby and open areas of the new wing.

While Vaughan talked to the Mayor for a moment, I pretended to sip my champagne while looking around at all of the other guests.

Then I saw a flash of nearly blinding fuchsia.

As the woman tottered in, clasping a thin, pale man's arm for dear life, I already had my suspicions of who it might be.

Every single thing about her seemed to be calculated to garner the most attention possible. Brassy bleached blonde hair, styled high with a smattering of gold clips. Her almost neon dress was cut both far too low and far too high in certain places while being far too tight everywhere else.

Glancing down, I could see why she was holding onto that man's arm so desperately. Her heels were so high I was genuinely shocked that she could walk at all.

Vaughan followed my stare and gripped my hand. "Yep, that's her."

I almost couldn't believe that Vaughan had ever been interested in such a woman. If she were dressed more appropriately, she might be pretty enough, I suppose.

But the expression on her face turned her appearance from pleasant to foul. Jessica was glaring daggers at every single person in the room while holding her head up as if she were some sort of deranged queen.

"Have I mentioned how grateful I am that you came with me tonight?" Vaughan asked, leaning down to nuzzle my ear. "I really am."

"I'm just glad that she has moved on and will stop trying to annoy you," I said. "A lot of women are desperate to marry a doctor. Apparently, she's landed one. Good for her."

Vaughan's jaw dropped, then he burst into laughter. "Damn, gorgeous, I've never heard you be catty before."

"I'm glad you caught that. I try not to let it out very often."

As we laughed together, I could almost feel Jessica's eyes on us but refused to look. I waited until the Mayor and his wife spun back around to tell us about their recent trip to Bermuda.

Out of the corner of my eye, I could see a flash of pink, then a blonde head swivel. I'd never felt so observed before, yet tried to keep the conversation flowing naturally. After a while, Jessica appeared to have wandered into one of the other rooms. At least the garish color made it easy to keep an eye on where she was.

"When do the toasts begin?" I asked Vaughan.

He checked his rather impressive watch. "Ten minutes or so."

"Perfect. I'll be back in a few minutes." I gave him a tiny kiss, which made his eyes sparkle.

I found the ladies' room to freshen up and check my lipstick, which thankfully wasn't smudged. I wasn't really listening to the other woman in the washroom until I heard a shrill voice call out from within one of the stalls. "Marcy, are you even listening to me?"

"Yes, Jessica. Settle down. You said you didn't want him anymore anyway," came the patient reply from the adjacent stall.

"Yes, but I still wanted to keep the option open, you know?"

"Vaughan was never the type to go for your Vegas wedding idea anyway."

"Who wouldn't want to get married in Las Vegas?" Jessica protested. "Maybe not by Elvis, but in one of those huge gold and white venues."

"Most people, actually," the voice that must have been Marcy replied. "Besides, you've got Doctor Kershaw now."

I heard a loud sigh. "Sure he's rich, but I don't know whether his salary is going to increase that much until at least ten years down the road. I don't know if it's going to be enough to give me my dream life, you know?"

"I think he has the most potential out of any of the men you've tried out over the past couple of years," Marcy said.

"Did you see that strange woman Vaughan is here with?" Jessica asked.

I fixed my hair and got ready to run.

"She's so unbelievably pretty," Marcy gushed. "She looks a bit like that princess from...where is it? That country where everyone is gorgeous? Anyway, someone said that's his new wife."

Darting out the door, I heard Jessica shriek, "*Wife?* What the hell?!"

I scurried back to Vaughan, grabbing us two fresh flutes of champagne along the way.

"I missed you," he whispered, brushing his lips across the top of my hair.

"As always, the ladies' room is gossip central," I whispered. "Jessica is concerned that her doctor won't be earning enough money for her imaginary perfect life, and her friend Marcy has informed her that we're married. Jessica...wasn't thrilled to hear it."

Vaughan grinned so hard it was almost unsettling. "Wonderful. Now she will finally stop calling and emailing the company, I hope."

"I hope so too," I said, finally allowing myself to take a real mouthful of champagne.

The official ceremonies and toasts were all going smoothly and then much to my surprise the Mayor called Vaughan up to the podium. I had no idea that he was going to be speaking.

"I didn't want to make you nervous," he said, giving me a kiss on the cheek while everyone stared over at us.

As he strode to the front of the room, he was followed by the eyes of many women who were also admiring how unbelievably hot he looked in that perfectly cut suit.

"Don't worry, this will be short, because I know we all

want to get back to these incredible snacks," Vaughan began, as people smiled appreciatively.

"I'd just like to thank the hospital board for selecting a slightly smaller construction company, and giving us this opportunity. Every time we hit a snag or delay, we thought about how this city deserves incredible medical care. Whenever we put in overtime, or missed a family function, we did it so that this hospital could expand on schedule to meet the needs of this amazing community. I'd like to thank my entire team for doing the most important job we've ever taken on. And of course, I'd like to thank my lovely wife Claudia for supporting me through thick and thin."

All eyes turned to me as Vaughan added, "That's it, thanks for coming, don't forget to hit the donation booth on the way out."

It was downright weird to have so many eyes on me as Vaughan came back over to kiss me right on the lips. It was light and sweet, but told everyone in the room exactly who I was to him.

I flung my left hand around his shoulder to let the ring sparkle in the light. Since Jessica and Marcy were definitely staring along with everyone else, there's no way they could have missed it.

The party picked back up again, and the conversation flowed more freely. I didn't mind as much when Vaughan and I were separated, now that I had been chatting with people for a while.

Ellen and some of her friends corralled me over near the dessert table. "That is a stunning ring," an older lady named Alice said, taking my hand to take a better look.

"Thank you," I replied, catching a flash of fuchsia in my peripheral vision just behind my left elbow. "Vaughan's mother and I get along so well that she insisted I have her fifth anniversary ring."

"You have to tell us about the wedding," Ellen grinned.

An arm slipped up my back as I felt Vaughan tuck into my right side.

"We didn't want a flashy, elaborate wedding," I said as the other women gathered closer. "Vaughan joked about going down to Vegas, but we all know how tacky that is, right, honey?" I laughed as I turned my head to look up at him.

The other women laughed with me, and I actually felt bad that Jessica was eavesdropping from right behind us. I definitely felt terrible for making fun of anyone's choice of wedding location, but my mission was to make Vaughan's ex realize we were permanent.

"So we rented a couple of huge cabins beside a breath-taking lake, since Vermont is the opposite of Vegas," I continued brightly. "Two of my friends are caterers, but we all pitched in to help under their direction. It was a lovely, relaxing weekend. Candlelight and wildflowers. Only twenty-two people, so we could actually talk to everyone."

"She was incredible," Vaughan said, looking down at me with more emotion than I expected. "Claudia organized everything. It all happened so smoothly we didn't even realize things were already taken care of. A local minister came by at sunset so that we could say our vows between the lake and the bonfire."

"That sounds so lovely. Plus, you must have saved a ton of money," Alice said.

"Oh, it wasn't about that," Vaughan said quickly. "We had a two-week honeymoon in Europe afterward. We just wanted to be able to sit down and hang out with our closest people without strangers buzzing around. You know how so many weddings have just hundreds of guests, and you end up hardly having a proper conversation with anyone?"

I wondered if that comment was directed to Jessica and Marcy, who were still close by.

"So, tell us about your family, dear," Ellen said. "I'm sure we must already know them."

That was the one question I had sincerely hoped wouldn't come up. Vaughan's hand was on my back and he clearly felt my shoulders stiffen.

"Actually, ladies, I need to sneak Claudia away for a moment, if you'll excuse us," he said. "We need to make a quick call to a friend right at ten."

We slipped out to a hallway, then down to an area with chairs. "I know you're getting tired," Vaughan said, sitting close beside me and draping my legs over his to raise my feet. "These are very cute shoes, but they must be starting to hurt."

"It's not too bad, but I'm starting to wonder how much longer we have left," I admitted.

"If we take a break now, can you hang on for just another half an hour?" he asked. "There are several important people I want to spend just a bit more time with."

"I'm happy to stay as long as you like," I said. "I was assuming several more hours. If it's an hour or less, my feet are going to be incredibly happy."

Vaughan leaned in to kiss me so gently that I was no longer caring about the lipstick. "I want you and your lovely feet to be incredibly happy at all times, gorgeous."

The way he caressed my calves was making me melt. We hadn't really discussed what was going to happen after the party, but I knew I didn't want this magical night to end. Ever.

**8**

---

## VAUGHAN

By the time I was slightly tipsy from the endless glasses of whiskey that were being pressed into my hand by the richest men in the city, I knew that the evening had been a total success. Claudia was definitely holding her own with all of the wives, and I had received more requests for job quotes in the past hour than I had in the past year.

There was no way to tell whether these were empty alcohol-inspired assurances, or definite work, but either way, if even just a few of them panned out, I might have to hire more crew.

All this time I thought my father had been gently suggesting I start dating more because he thought I was lonely. I honestly had no idea that being married was also good for business.

Even the few gentlemen who were divorced were still viewed a different way than those who had never been married. It was all extremely strange to me, but since it was working in my favor, I wasn't going to rock the boat.

I was just beginning to start saying my goodbyes when

Chester Oxford pulled me aside. He was a massive developer who always had dozens of projects on the go.

"Vaughan, Francine thinks that your wife Claudia is absolutely precious. We've been thinking about adding a younger couple to our monthly barbecues."

Since he was one of the richest men in the city, with an estate that was almost as large as some palaces, I could well imagine what his parties must be like.

"Plus, we could have a chat about sliding you some work," Chester said with a wink. "We always like to give good work to good people. You know how it is."

"Absolutely. I'd love to be considered. Thank you so much."

"I'll call you later this week as soon as Francine sets the date of our next bash," he said. "But I'm pretty sure it's in two weeks."

I shook his hand, then looked around for Claudia. Good Lord. She had been cornered by Jessica and Marcy near the dessert table.

Practically sprinting across the room, I arrived just in time to hear Marcy say, "Don't be a bitch, Jessica. It's not her fault Vaughan's Mom didn't like you."

"Hey, baby," I said, wrapping a protective arm around Claudia. "The driver is waiting out front. Let's get you off your feet."

I could see the relief in her eyes as she nodded. "Sure." Turning to the other women, she said, "Lovely to meet you both. Have a good evening."

She sounded so sweet and sincere and I was impressed by her acting abilities. Maybe I was an ass for not greeting Jessica at all, but I didn't see the need.

The second we were around the corner, I sent our driver a text. "I lied about the car, sorry, gorgeous. He'll be here in one minute. But I didn't want you to be stuck with them for another second."

There was a slight commotion down the hall, as I saw a few latecomers were arriving and being greeted by the Hospital Director. I recognized a guy who was running in this fall's Mayoral election, and a couple of bank presidents.

"Did you want to go meet the guy who might become our next Mayor?" I asked.

Claudia shook her head firmly. "Honestly, I'd rather not, but I'm happy to wait if you need to. Sorry."

"No, let's get out of here." As soon as we were safely in the back of the car, I slipped her shoes off and began to rub her feet. "So, what did Jessica say?" I asked.

Claudia rolled her eyes. "Vaughan, I'm sorry, I know she's your ex, but that woman is unbelievable. She expected me to tell her how much your net worth has increased over the past two years, and where I expected it to be in ten. Who thinks like that?"

She moaned as I dug my thumb into her arches. The feeling of caring for her was stirring up another wave of feelings for my sweet girl.

"I know. My poor sweet wife. I'm sorry you had to deal with this."

"It was actually sort of enlightening," she said. "Some of those women have fascinating careers. Others are mothers and homemakers, which is equally important. But then some of them..." She shook her head, causing a few loose tendrils of hair to fall out of her twist. "It honestly sounds like all they do is shop and travel."

"Don't you like shopping?"

Claudia held out her hand, seesawing it back and forth. "It depends what for. Dropping by the veggie market is fun.

Having to buy a bunch of new clothes for work in a few weeks...not so fun."

"Well, I appreciate that you shopped for me," I said, pulling her into my lap. "You have no idea what it did to me watching you in this lovely dress all night. It was almost as beautiful as you."

Kissing down her throat, I pulled the fabric down an inch to kiss along the edge of her breast. Her breathing became uneven, and I loved how responsive she was.

"I guess I'll have to hang up this dress until I'm invited to an upscale party with an entirely different group of people," she laughed. "Oh – and let me give you back the ring, before I forget."

Grabbing her hand, I held the ring in place. "When I gave this to you, you agreed to be my wife for the night."

"Yes...?" Her eyebrow raised.

"What do you think about coming back to my place?" I asked, as softly and gently as possible.

She bit her bottom lip, thinking. "Well, that depends. Some men have a whole lot of expectations of their wives."

"I have no expectations. Only a deep desire to hold you against me for as long as you'll let me."

Claudia paused, those beautiful eyes sparkling. "In that case, my husband, yes."

I tapped on the window between us and the driver so that he'd lower it an inch. "My house. Thanks."

"Yes, sir."

The first time we were at my house, it was all about getting to know each other so that we could pretend to have been living together in case anyone asked a pointed question. This time my only mission was to get to know Claudia in a more intimate way.

As soon as we were inside, I helped her slip off her

shoes, then scooped her up in my arms. "My beautiful princess wife, where would you like to go?"

"Well, I don't know. What are my options?" she asked coyly.

"If you're hungry, we can go to the kitchen and I'll fix you something. If you want to chill out and watch a movie, I'll get you comfy on the couch and just make you some tea."

"So far. so good. Is there an option three?"

The second her gaze locked onto mine, I knew where we were headed. "Or I could take you to the bedroom, get you out of this dress, beautiful as it is, and kiss every single inch of my ravishing wife."

Her tongue darted out across her lips nervously, then she nodded. "Bedroom."

I've never held such precious cargo as I walked slowly upstairs.

Claudia had been absolutely bewitching all evening. Now it was time for me to show her how much I truly cared about her when we were alone, not when she was on display as my fake wife.

Although the more time I spent with her, the more I was convinced that we truly belonged together. It was only a matter of time before I made her my wife for real.

**9**

___________

## CLAUDIA

I'd never known a man to be so attentive. Even when Vaughan had been wheeling and dealing with those important people, he was always keeping an eye on me at the same time.

It made me feel safe in a way I'd never experienced. And now, the way he held me as he carried me upstairs made me feel treasured.

The way Vaughan had stared at me all night made me shiver. I didn't think I was that pretty at all, but he genuinely thought I was beautiful. His oddly intense gaze made my body tingle and tense. My nipples were aching from having been stiff all night in the unfamiliar strapless bra.

Feeling Vaughan's hands on the back of my thighs as he carried me wasn't enough. I wanted to feel them everywhere.

The bedroom was ultra modern, in gray and silver, with the exception of a pair of hand carved wooden nightstands on either side of the massive bed. He set me on my feet, and I stared up into those gorgeous green eyes.

As he dipped his head to kiss me, I placed a hand in the center of his chest. "Lipstick. Hold on."

Darting to the washroom, I was still carrying my little purse that had a few special wipes the makeup artist had given me. I quickly cleaned my lips and removed the false lashes before returning to Vaughan.

He had taken off his shoes, socks, and jacket, but still looked stunning. Something about that crisp, formal jacket stretching across his shoulders had been triggering my lust all night long.

"Mmm, that's better," he said, pulling me against him to absolutely ravage my mouth. It was as if he had been starving for me. Perhaps that was a good trick to remember – by denying him real kisses for most of the night, now he seemed nearly out of control.

Then he turned me away from him, his fingers hovering at the three tiny crystal hooks that held the back of my dress together.

"May I?"

"Yes," I whispered.

The back of my neck prickled in anticipation as he unfastened the dress and my bra, sliding everything to the floor in one fluid motion. His hands settled on my hips as he kissed along the back of my shoulder. He slipped out the clip so that my hair tumbled down, and I hoped it had landed in a sexy mess.

Even the simplest of touches zinged straight through me, increasing my desire until I felt like I might shatter if he were to stop.

I'd never had such a clear, concrete realization before. I wanted him. Completely.

Turning in his arms, I reached up to grab him by the hair, pulling his lips down to mine to kiss him hungrily.

He released me just long enough to remove his tie. My hands flew up to start unbuttoning his shirt without thought. Maybe I really was becoming bolder. Or maybe my body was finally kicking my mind out of the way and taking what it needed.

As I slipped off his shirt, I barely managed to hold back a tiny choked noise. His torso was a beautiful sculpture I knew already I would never be able to explore enough. My fingers danced across every curve and dip, as my mouth pressed to the center of his chest.

"Claudia," he murmured huskily, "I need to taste you."

It wasn't quite clear whether he meant it as a command or a request, but I nodded, sitting down on the bed and crawling backward.

Vaughan lay over me, sucking my nipple between his lips until I squealed. He knew precisely when to be gentle, and when to be firm. I almost giggled when I realized the head of a construction company would know all about balance of all kinds.

His sexy mouth brushed against mine again as he murmured, "I've been wanting to check something all night, gorgeous."

His hand skimmed down my stomach to dip into my panties, where I'd been wet from the second he picked me up in the front hallway. As that thick middle finger dragged slowly through my crease, I moaned loudly.

"Mmm, baby, you're soaked."

Gasping, I nodded. "Yes."

He kissed me again, his tongue caressing mine as his finger lightly explored my most sensitive skin. His other hand closed around my breast, making me whimper as my back arched, eager to place myself in his hands. Feeling

Vaughan's powerful body over mine made me feel delicate. As if I somehow contrasted against his strength.

My hips began to wriggle, eagerly moving my pussy against his finger so that it would brush against my clit. I looked up to see Vaughan's eyes clenched, almost as if he were in pain.

"You're so sexy. I've never been anywhere near a woman as gorgeous as you are, and this...the way you're moving. The way we're so hot for each other. It's almost more than I can stand, baby."

His next kiss was molten. Almost dangerous. Gasping against his mouth, I wondered if it was possible to pass out from being so aroused.

Then he kissed a path lower, swirling and looping around my breasts, taking time to feast on each nipple slowly before moving lower.

He slipped off my panties, spreading my legs as he settled himself between them. My core tightened as his rough hands slipped up my inner thighs. It felt like he was quivering with anticipation as well.

His thumb slipped gently along the grooves at the very top of my legs, teasing me before moving inward. My abdomen compressed as I tried to stop my hips from moving as he ran his thumbs along my labia while staring into my naked pussy.

Words completely failed me as he nudged me open, then dragged a fingertip slowly around my clit. His gentle touch left me breathless and overheated, as he explored me softly, as if every inch of me was the most delicate fine china.

"So beautiful," he murmured.

Vaughan turned his head to scrape his teeth along my inner thigh, making me whimper. Then he darted forward to drop his mouth to my center, kissing and lapping until I couldn't control my noises anymore. His hot breath against my wet skin, the stroke of his tongue circling my entrance, every single touch, made my entire body quiver helplessly.

I'd never felt empty before, but as soon as his thick middle finger began to slip inside, I had a deep need to be filled. Vaughan's lips latched onto my clit, sucking and licking as he began to stroke deeper.

"I need you soaking wet, baby," he murmured as those dazzling green eyes stared up at me. "Can you be a good little wife for me and come on my tongue?"

Why did his words cause my mind to disintegrate? Because he kept calling me his wife, or because he was talking dirty to me when I was already so close to the edge?

Goosebumps were prickling my arms as I reached down to grip his hair, holding his mouth tightly against me.

Somehow I wasn't even embarrassed by my desperation. My body had taken control and was completely in charge. I had no idea that a climax with a man would be a thousand times more intense than the few times I'd tried on my own.

I loved that Vaughan was older, with more life experience. I loved how he took control. And I was nearly delirious from realizing that I was already completely in love with him.

His eyes blazed as he lapped harder, digging in as his finger moved faster, deeper. His other hand gripped my hip, holding me still as I could no longer control my squirming.

"Please," I begged shamelessly, not even knowing what I wanted. "Please."

His tongue raked over my swollen button more steadily as he realized I was getting close. My breath came out in irregular pants as I clutched his hair, staring deeply into his eyes.

Vaughan winked, giving me the tiniest nod as I pitched forward, squealing and gasping as I stared at him, nearly hypnotized as I began to climax. Everything pulled inward, so tight, so hot, before exploding outward in a rush.

"Yes," I managed to rasp as he opened me with a second finger exactly as I peaked, shaking as the waves tumbled over and through me.

He continued licking steadily until I collapsed back against the bed. Kissing his way back up, I needed his lips on mine. With a start, I realized I needed more. Everything.

Reaching for his belt, my few clumsy tugs told him what I wanted.

"Are you sure, baby?" he asked softly.

"Absolutely."

Although the way we were lost in each other's eyes was completely serious, I still felt the need to keep things light. "I want to be a good wife for you, after all."

Vaughan chuckled as he stood up, slipping off the rest of his clothes and making me shudder with anticipation. The thick, stiff shaft was nestled perfectly between his powerful thighs, and bobbed as he came to lie over me.

"Should I get a con—"

"I'm on the pill," I blurted at the same time as he spoke. Somehow, laughing together at such a gigantic moment took the edge off.

The head of his massive cock slipped back and forth between my soaking pussy lips. I wasn't sure whether he was teasing us both, or lubricating his skin.

All I knew was that as his lips clung to mine and he began to shift, sinking inside me just a bit, I felt changed. Not only was it my first time having sex, but it was my first time feeling this torrent of warmth, trust, and desire for another person.

I was absolutely in love with Vaughan. Although I couldn't quite find the words to say it yet, I hoped that he felt it in the way my hands gripped the back of his shoulders, my tongue danced with his, and my body opened to welcome him inside.

**10**

---

# VAUGHAN

**M**y ears were ringing slightly. My blood ran icy hot, as if I were feverish. I'd never felt lust like this before, but that didn't begin to describe everything that was happening.

I could see it in Claudia's eyes. She had dropped that shield around herself, the outgoing personality that she felt she had to use with everybody else. Now she was real. Sweet and vulnerable and ready to savor every second of this experience with me.

At the second I realized I was already completely in love with her, she was thinking the same thing. It was so clear in those wide blue eyes.

Her thighs tightened as she tipped herself up to me, and we moaned together as I sunk into her soft, wet sweetness just half an inch.

"Easy, baby. I don't want to hurt you."

"It's okay," she said, closing her eyes as if she couldn't bear to meet mine as she whispered, "I know it'll only be for a minute."

Oh my God. This breathtakingly gorgeous girl was a

virgin? And she already felt so close to me that she was ready for this? To give herself to me completely?

Maybe I should have stopped to discuss the matter further, but as her eyes opened, blazing into mine, there was no mistaking that she wanted me every bit as much as I wanted her.

"Tell me to stop if it's too much, sweetheart," I whispered, entering her snug passage as slowly as possible.

She shifted and wiggled against me, then made a strange whining squeak before gasping. Slowly I pressed deeper, her tight tunnel walls squeezing me so hard it was the most intense thing I'd ever felt.

Her body opened up to mine as I kissed across her forehead. Then I paused to let her adjust to the intrusion, even though remaining still felt completely unnatural to me in this moment.

"Breathe, gorgeous." I kissed her gently, then looked down into those lovely eyes as she gasped. "Relax, baby. You're the most precious person in the entire world to me, do you know that?"

Claudia's blinked in surprise, then whispered, "I feel the same way about you."

"Good. Do you want more?"

She began to nod, but I caught her lips in a dreamy, breathless kiss as I slowly thrust deeper. Her tongue felt skittish against mine as her body quivered, her fingers dancing restlessly across my shoulders.

I could feel a bead of sweat roll down my back, the effort required to move so slowly making everything tense up. Claudia shifted her hips again, tilting to help me press deeper. Suddenly something within her opened up and I sank into her softness while we both moaned.

"Oh!" she gasped against my mouth as I kissed her harder, deeper.

"Do you like that, baby? Do you want more?"

"Yes," she moaned, as her eyelids flickered as if unable to open. "More."

I felt my cock throbbing inside her as I began to take long, slow strokes. Another wave of her sweet juices released, bathing my cock in her wetness, easing the way. I pulled out, only to push back in, filling her completely.

"Wow," she muttered. "This is incredible."

It felt like my insides were twisting as I forced myself to hold back. "Wrap your legs around my waist. Open wide and relax, sweetheart."

Claudia did as I asked, then it felt like her entire body was surrendering to mine. Watching her eyes, I could see the moment she discovered that if she tilted a certain way, I moved against her clit with every stroke.

Scooping my hands under her back, I helped her arch against me as we moved together, then apart, finding a rhythm where we ignited every nerve, over and over.

"Vaughan," she gasped, her fingertips digging into my flesh as she trembled, "I think..."

"That's it, baby," I said while tilting her head back to kiss along her throat. "Let go."

The pressure of my impending climax was building swiftly, yet I was determined to hold on until Claudia came.

Just as I was about to bring my fingers down to her swollen little button to help send her over the edge, she gasped louder, her head writhing from side to side as her unbelievably tight pussy began to clench around me.

"Vaughan," she cried. "Faster. Please."

It felt like thunder and lightning were rattling my insides as I moved faster, quick pumps of my cock filling her smoothly but quickly. Our breathing was ragged, the bed almost shaking as I drove harder.

Claudia's head fell back with a wail that echoed through the room as I felt the release flooding her sexy body. Her porcelain skin flushed as her mouth fell open.

I loved her. This beautiful girl who trusted me so completely, and chose me to care for her. I loved this thoughtful, precious woman who alternated between shy and bold, sassy and brilliant.

Losing myself completely, I almost didn't hear myself chanting her name as I kissed her, clutching her desperately against me as I possessed her completely. Her thighs flexed around me as I pounded into her slick pussy, both of us shaking as the clenching of her tunnel walls pushed me over the cliff.

I came with a roar, flooding her to overflowing as I released. Lights seemed to flicker at the edge of my vision as I tried to focus on the beautiful face staring up at me.

Kissing her gently, we both whispered, "Wow," at the same time, then laughed together.

Finally I stopped moving, just holding her for a minute or two before our hot, panting breaths smoothed out. Then I rolled onto my side, gathering her close in my arms. Running my fingertips along her hairline, I kissed the tip of her nose.

I had to tell her how I felt. Yet the long ingrained fear of admitting feelings too soon held me back.

"I love absolutely everything about you," I finally whispered, hoping that would convey my meaning without quite making the declaration outright.

Claudia nodded, and I could see that she instantly knew what I meant. "I was thinking exactly the same thing," she said softly.

We curled up together so comfortably it was as if our bodies were made for each other. I would never tire of holding this gorgeous woman in my arms. It was almost difficult to fall asleep because I didn't want to miss a single second of her pressed up against me.

We fit together so perfectly in every possible way that I already knew we were permanent. It was just a matter of time before she would no longer just be playing the role of my wife. I could not wait to watch her walking down the aisle toward me, no matter where we ended up making it official.

## 11

## CLAUDIA

I briefly woke up a few times in the night to feel Vaughan's arms wrapped around me. Feeling so utterly cared for even while I was asleep was lovely.

I'd always been independent, and being on my own was wonderful, but having someone else to rely on let me relax in an entirely new way. I didn't know if it was too soon, but I wanted to get used to the constant feeling of being safe when he was around.

When I woke up with sunshine streaming through the crack between the curtains, I could sense that Vaughan wasn't in the room even before my eyes fully opened. Rolling over and stretching, I heard the distinct crinkle of a plastic bag. Sitting up, there was something at the foot of the bed.

I dug in to find yoga pants, a baggy long-sleeved t-shirt, and flip-flops, all in various shades of dark blue. Plus two pairs of strangely-cut cotton underwear that were white with pink flowers.

After a quick shower, I borrowed Vaughan's mouthwash and found scissors in his bathroom drawer to cut the tags off the new clothing. Plus I couldn't resist checking the water level of the new Boston fern. Then I went down to find him humming to himself in the kitchen.

"Good morning, gorgeous," his deep voice purred. He quickly washed his hands, drying them on his worn jeans before returning to me.

Vaughan shirtless and barefoot in light blue jeans was a sight I would carry with me until the end of my days. The deep grooves cut over his hips. The rippled six pack. The sculpted shoulders and slightly rounded biceps, even when he wasn't flexing. And those dark green eyes – that was what made my heart flutter most of all.

He kissed me gently, snuggling me against him. "I hope the clothes are all right. The dollar store was the only place open this early on a Sunday. I could've just given you a t-shirt to wear around the house, but you're going to need some kind of pants to get home eventually."

"You went out and shopped for me?"

"Of course."

Kissing him again, I murmured, "You are unbelievably sweet."

"So are you. And so is vanilla hazelnut coffee."

He kissed the top of my head, then pointed to the kitchen table. I'd never dreamed of having such a gorgeous man serve me coffee, fruit, toast, and eggs. Heck – I'd never even dreamed of being in such a nice house.

My mother had done her best, but we were always in tiny apartments. Dad had deserted us when I was just eight, before he started wheeling and dealing in business and politics, and started making actual money. Even when it did start rolling in for him, we of course never saw a penny of it.

Eating and chatting and washing dishes with Vaughan was so blissfully comfortable, as if we'd been together months instead of a week. As if we already knew that this was forever, and that we belonged together.

We hadn't really discussed the details, but it was clear this relationship was going to continue, even without the fake marriage.

It had been ages since I'd just hung out with someone for long periods of time. Chatting about everything and nothing. Letting the conversation wander in big, lazy loops as we shared both the wonderful and mundane details of each other's lives.

All the while, it was clear to both of us that we were falling head over heels in love.

Vaughan told me about his extensive team, and how they worked with various architects and engineers to create all sorts of structures.

I obviously avoided speaking about my family, but shared how much I loved writing promotional content for companies. It was incredible to see how excited people were about their projects and businesses. Translating what they wanted to say into bite-size content suitable for the web was an interesting challenge.

That's why I liked it. It was, as my grandmother used to say, persnickety. Fussy and detailed and the sort of thing I frankly loved getting lost in for hours at a time.

It felt good to share the details of my life with someone. It was also wonderful how intently Vaughan listened to me.

After we finished the brunch dishes, we went to sit in his beautiful backyard with another cup of coffee. There was so much space out here that I couldn't help wondering if he'd ever thought of children. There was a perfect open spot for a swing set or jungle gym.

"How many more classes do you have left?" he asked.

"I sent in the last paper for one class last week," I said.

"Then I have one more paper for an English literature course, then that's it, I'm done."

"So you have a couple of weeks of summer vacation, right? You said you start your new job at the beginning of October?"

"Yes."

"Good. Would you mind playing my wife again for a barbecue at the Oxfords' mansion?"

"Sure." I waved the emerald and diamond ring at him. "It'll give me another excuse to wear this for a night." Vaughan chuckled as I added, "You really do need to give me the ring box so that we can put this away. I certainly can't wear it to work."

His lips pressed together as he looked down for a moment. "My first thought is that I'd like you to wear it so that other men know that you're taken. Is that terrible of me?"

"Not terrible, no. Maybe...a bit *much* so soon, but I know it's in a well-intended way. You know what I mean?"

"Good." He reached out to hold my hand. "I always want to be incredibly honest with you, Claudia. I know it's completely nuts in some ways, but I feel like we're already permanent. I almost don't want to say that in case I freak you out, but somehow I just know that we are already a done deal."

There was no way I could express the nervousness that gripped my core at the same time. Or the fear that he would find out that I wasn't actually right for him. Lowering my voice, I only whispered, "I have the same feeling. I'm just afraid to say it out loud."

Vaughan squeezed my hand as he grinned, then said, "As we were saying, this coffee is fabulous."

My laughter rang out across the patio. "You know, now

that you are a stable married man, you might have to throw some of your own shindigs and events. You've got a great space for them."

His fingers threaded through mine as his thumb began to rub in little circles against my skin. "Thank goodness I have an incredible wife who will help me with things like party planning," he said with a grin. "I certainly don't know anything about that."

"What's to know? Food, drinks, a selection of interesting people with a few things in common. Plus triple the amount of ice that you'll think you'll need."

Apparently my genius ice trick sent him over the edge, as I was suddenly lifted and dropped into his lap.

I loved the way he kissed me. The way he grazed his soft lips against mine so gently, then plundered my mouth in a deep, delicious kiss that stole my breath and made my mind fuzzy with desire.

By the time he pulled away, I was wondering whether it would be too forward to take him back upstairs again.

"You mentioned that you still have a bit of schoolwork to get done today. I still have a few hours of paperwork to go through myself. So I'm going to drive you home so that we can be responsible, productive people. Okay?"

"Okay. Good idea."

Vaughan leaned in to nibble along the side of my neck. "But I'm going to be pestering you for both hangouts and official dates as much as possible."

"Good."

Even the drive home was fun as we sang along to a fifties rock station.

After a goodbye kiss that lasted ten minutes but was still too short, I went up to my apartment with my glamorous dress and shoes rolled carefully in some cloth shopping bags. Once I'd put them away, I realized something important.

I was still wearing his mother's ring. Every time I tried to give it back, Vaughan didn't want me to.

How strange that it felt like I had a permanent connection to him, just from wearing something that he had given me.

Wearing a token of his affection made me his, and even if it was a symbol of a relationship step we were nowhere near taking yet, I wasn't going to remove it for anything.

## 12

# VAUGHAN

As I left work on Wednesday evening, my head was practically spinning. Some of my new ultra rich contacts wanted estimates and proposals for buildings, which was great. The thing was, though, they wanted information immediately, even if the project might not break ground for three years.

I had decided the fabulously wealthy were also fabulously impatient.

I stayed late to arrange things so that my team could at least start feeding them little bits of information to keep them satisfied while we pulled together all of the details.

When I finally got into my truck, a wave of relief washed over me. I would never have to come out here and see Jessica lurking around the vehicle again. I'd never leave the office and have her waiting for me in the lobby. I hadn't realized how much her pestering and loitering had annoyed me.

Even though it hadn't happened for at least two months, there was always the worry that she'd come back. Yet now I knew she was gone for good, and it was a bigger relief than I had expected. Having someone breathing down your neck was downright creepy, whether they were harmless or not.

Before I started driving, I grabbed my phone to send Claudia a text.

**Me:** Have a great shift tonight, baby. I'll be by at 11 to pick you up.

**Claudia:** I appreciate it, but you don't have to drive me home every single night. Really, the bus is fine.

**Me:** Well, I'm available tonight, so I'm going to. I'm a terrible husband. Smothering you already.

**Claudia:** Just the worst. LOL. I really appreciate it, honey.

I knew she was just teasing when she called me honey, but I couldn't help but feel a warm pang in the center of my chest every time she did.

I felt so good to be with her. Claudia was so easygoing that it was natural to imagine being married to her, and with her for the rest of my life.

On the drive home I thought about all of my favorite restaurants in the city, and how I was going to start taking her there one by one.

There was still so much to learn about her. Did she like going out to restaurants several times a week? Or was once enough? She seemed to be very comfortable in the kitchen, so maybe she would like to cook together every Sunday?

Since we both had busy schedules, I was already thinking about creating rituals with her, carving out time together that we could always look forward to. In some ways I knew that I was counting my chickens before they were hatched, but everything about our relationship seemed to be on fast forward.

The smile on my face completely dissolved when I

pulled into my driveway and had to park on the left since someone else's car was on the right.

Jessica. What an instantaneous way to ruin my evening.

I got out of the car and went around to her open driver side window. She was wearing bright blue eyeshadow that almost matched her car.

"Hey there, Vaughan," she purred as she clicked her long purple fingernails against the steering wheel.

I had noticed that her nails matched her dress on Saturday night. How often did women get manicures, anyway?

"Why are you here, Jessica?"

She stuck out her bottom lip in a dramatic pout. "Can't a girl just pop by to check on a super close friend?"

"No. Especially when I've asked you repeatedly to please leave me alone."

"Well, we used to be very close," she said with a wink.

"It was so long ago I can barely remember it," I said coldly. "I'll ask you again, why are you here?"

She rolled her eyes dramatically. "I was just wondering whether you thought your underhanded little scheme was really going to go unnoticed?"

Of all of the people to potentially find out that Claudia and I weren't really married, Jessica would be the absolute worst case scenario. Forcing my face to remain perfectly neutral, I said, "What on earth are you talking about?"

She grinned widely, looking like the cat who just ate the canary. "I can't believe that you didn't mention the truth about your new wife," she said slowly. "But don't worry. I understand using relationships to try to get ahead."

"You certainly do," I said flatly. "The entire city knows that you're an opportunistic gold digger. You might as well have it tattooed across your forehead."

I knew that was mean but I couldn't stop myself. She had gotten under my skin for so long that I didn't have the energy to be polite any longer.

"Yes, but you already have money," she said smoothly. "So now you're after power and connections, apparently."

"I was at the hospital opening because we built the wing," I said as if explaining it to a three year old. "Of course I was going to socialize with people there. What are you trying to say?"

"Just that your new wife seems to have been selected very carefully," Jessica said.

My blood turned to ice. My heart began to beat in that slow, off-kilter rhythm they used in movies when the killer could be around any corner.

"So you don't like Claudia," I said with what I hoped was a casual shrug. "You don't like most women. Why don't you go home and think about why that might be?"

"Oh no, you don't understand," she said, shaking her head as she ran a hand through the carefully-arranged waves in her hair. "I actually admire her. Once her father is the Mayor, and she has her hooks into a construction company, she can build her own little empire."

I blinked hard, not sure what she was trying to say.

"Or of course, if she's busy with her own hobbies," Jessica continued, "she could simply take both your money, and her father's money, and shop and travel as much as she wants."

She flashed me an exaggerated wink. "Honestly, I really do admire the girl." Jessica reached out to hand me a pink and white business card. "Could you please give that to Claudia? I would just love to take her out to lunch. I need to know her secrets, not just how to lock down a wealthy man so fast, but also how she manages to make everyone like her instantly. Tell her she can pick the restaurant."

Jessica slipped on a pair of oversized sunglasses, then started the engine and drove away.

Stomping into the house, I made myself a quick dinner while trying to figure out what the hell Jessica had been talking about.

Through our mini conversations about her family, Claudia had mentioned that she wasn't very close with her mother, and her father had left when she was young. Was he rich? Why would Jessica think that I even knew the guy? And what did she mean about when her father became Mayor?

After catching up on some paperwork, I grabbed my phone to text Claudia that I was on the way. As I saw her name in my contacts, it finally clicked.

Claudia Lorimer. Pierce Lorimer was running for Mayor.

An avalanche of recollections tumbled around my mind at once. I had joked about Claudia being related to him when I had seen the promo poster at the beach, but she'd changed the subject immediately instead of laughing with me.

She didn't want to go meet the potential new Mayor at the hospital opening. I hadn't thought anything of it at the time, just that my poor sweetheart needed to get off her feet.

Could it actually be that she was avoiding her Dad because she didn't want a scene, or to be seen with him? Why was Claudia ashamed to be associated with him? My heart sank as I considered another possibility – that maybe her father had been cruel to her and her mother, and she never wanted to see him again. I really hoped that wasn't the case.

Dammit. I could see why Jessica would think it was

some sort of calculated move on my part to marry the daughter of a man who might be coming into power in the area where I did business.

Even though I personally thought that alliances like that usually ranged from sketchy to downright criminal, it was the way her mind always worked.

The only way to find out the truth was to speak to Claudia.

I walked into Ray's Diner just as Claudia and Scotty were locking up. He was shoving her playfully in the arm as she pretended to steal the keys, but stopped the second I approached.

"Is my girl being a naughty troublemaker again?" I asked him. "If so, I'm here to help keep her in line."

He smiled as soon as he realized I wasn't threatened by their work friendship. "She's a constant source of both amusement and annoyance," he said with a huff.

"You desperately need both," Claudia said with a laugh. "Scotty, this is Vaughan."

We shook hands, then I said, "Have a good night."

He waved, and I helped her into the truck. "Thank you so much for coming to get me," she said.

"No problem. It'll give us a chance to talk about the strangest conversation I had a few hours ago."

She looked puzzled, but I didn't want to have this chat while driving. I waited until we were parked in front of her building to turn to her.

I quickly ran through Jessica appearing at my house, and her assumption that either Claudia married me to forge a powerful connection between my company and her father, or that I married Claudia in order to get in her father's good graces.

The more I spoke, the paler Claudia became. I took her

hands, kissing the back of each of them. "I'm not angry," I said gently. "I don't give a damn what Jessica thinks. I just want to know the truth."

Claudia's eyes were swimming with tears.

"Please don't cry, baby. I'm just confused why you wouldn't tell me."

She stared out the window as if trying to get her bearings, giving me time to think of something truly horrific.

"Claudia, you didn't think this was a temporary relationship, did you? Did you keep this from me because you didn't think I'd ever find out? That we'd be together for that short a time?"

Staring into those beautiful blue eyes as tears began to stream down her cheeks, I suddenly felt lost.

I was already in love with this fascinating girl. If she hadn't actually been taking things seriously, and I'd been misreading absolutely everything, I honestly didn't know what I'd do.

## 13

## CLAUDIA

It was one of my biggest fears. That the outgoing, bubbly personality I pulled on every day like a comfy sweater would completely unravel.

How on earth could I have thought that I could hide such a thing from Vaughan? Of course he was going to find out who my father was eventually. If we were going to pretend to be married, or actually have our real relationship progress, he would ask more questions someday, and he would deserve answers.

The thought of Vaughan knowing that I was related to such a shady character actually turned my stomach.

Pulling my hands away, they balled into fists as I gripped my skirt. Shame and deep sadness began to overwhelm me. My hopes for this promising, wonderful new relationship were shattered.

"I'm sorry," I sniffled, digging in my purse for a tissue. "I haven't spoken to him in years. I was hoping that he would move away or at least lay low for a while."

"So he really is your father?" Vaughan asked.

"Yes. It's horrible. I know that you can't possibly have your reputation connected to his in any way."

"Baby, I didn't say that. I just want to know what's going on so that we can figure out how to handle it."

I shook my head firmly after wiping my eyes. "You have a good, steady, family company. I can't possibly jeopardize that in any way."

"We're not quite that fragile," Vaughan said with a tight smile. "Besides, people might not even connect the dots."

"If a twit like Jessica can figure it out, anyone can," I snapped, then clapped a hand over my mouth. "I'm sorry. I'm just...absolutely humiliated to be connected to him, even if it's in name only. He has bankrupted people before. Dealt with really dangerous people. He's poisonous, and I don't want him in my life at all."

"Then he won't be," Vaughan said smoothly. "Just let me take care of it."

"No. Absolutely not." I slipped off my seatbelt and squared my shoulders. "This is not your problem, Vaughan. You need to work on all of your new connections, and making your family proud. I don't factor into any of that."

"Claudia, I—"

"No," I said firmly. "I'm not going to be the one to ruin your father's legacy, your family's reputation. People will probably forget they even met me in a couple of months, then I can be gone from your life."

"Please, baby, just—"

"Let me go," I begged. "This is hard enough as it is, Vaughan. Please just give me a clean break and don't make it worse."

As I grabbed my purse, the emerald and diamond ring sparkled from my finger. Slipping it off, I dropped it into his palm, unable to meet his eyes.

I jumped out of the truck, not giving him time to come around and help me down. It was worth nearly twisting my ankle to get away. I knew that if he held me in those thick arms for even a second, my resolve might falter. My body craved his for comfort, and I didn't want to be weak.

As soon as I was in my apartment with the door locked behind me, I fell into a heap on the couch, my sobs shaking the pieces of my broken heart.

I'd been so focused on pretending everything was going to be perfect that I hadn't thought things through. My outgoing personality was great for work, but it wasn't strong enough to last forever,

It didn't matter now. It was over. Vaughan would certainly never forgive me for potentially embarrassing him, and for running away like a scared child. He couldn't risk everything for me. I certainly wasn't worth it.

He needed someone who could help him a lot more than I ever could. Someone who could be on committees, and mingle with those women who seemed obsessed with talking about their husbands.

That wasn't really the life for me anyway. I just wanted to be with Vaughan. If puzzle pieces don't fit, you can't force them. They'll only break.

FOR THE NEXT THREE DAYS, I ignored Vaughan's calls and texts. Luckily he didn't come to the diner, or I might have fallen apart. Bob and Taylor acted as if everything was fine, which made me want to cry all over again.

All I had to do was hold it together for another week, and train my replacement. Then maybe see if I could try to have some summer fun by myself before I started my new job.

I should be excited for the new chapter, but I was totally numb. Every single thing in my life would be better if Vaughan were with me.

But I wouldn't be like my father. I wouldn't selfishly put my needs above others'. The last thing I ever wanted was to be like him in any way.

No. Keeping my distance from Vaughan was the kindest, most logical thing I could possibly do. Even if it tore me apart in the process.

## 14

## VAUGHAN

I wanted to give Claudia some space, so I forced myself not to send her any messages Thursday morning. It seemed to me like her reaction was quite a bit bigger than it should have been, but I didn't know all the facts.

So I resorted to what I always did when I wasn't sure about something: I called in an expert.

After putting every scrap of information I had into a rambling email, I sent it to my researcher, Theo. He had an entire team who did data analysis on all sorts of things before we ever broke ground on a project.

Yet he had implied several times that he had an extensive staff who were happy to look into other sorts of matters, should the need arise.

After working all afternoon on a backbreaking but under the circumstances therapeutic small demolition job, I left the rest of the team to clean up the debris while I went to my home office.

A short piping hot shower to soothe my shoulders and a quick coffee later, I sat down at my laptop. As always, Theo had gone above and beyond the call.

It turned out that Pierce Lorimer was a conniving bastard of the highest order. There was a meandering laundry list of businesses he had joined, promising to help, then bankrupted through his bizarre business practices, not least of which was his habit of giving himself ridiculous bonuses and perks.

He somehow managed to leave every city on a high note every few years, so that he could blindside the next round of investors.

And now he was here, attempting a second time to run for Mayor. From what Theo had gathered online, nobody in Kingsville was falling for his bullshit, and his popularity ratings were abysmal.

Yet it was true that being associated with this man in any way would indeed be bad for my reputation.

It didn't concern me in the least. The only thing that mattered was Claudia.

Skimming the list of Pierce's associates here, none of them was in the top tier of business people. They weren't the powerful heads of advisory boards and presidents of banks that I was now getting to know.

Pierce wasn't a threat, and it genuinely looked like he was going to go out with a whimper, not a bang.

So – problem solved. But how was I going to get Claudia to listen to me? My poor sweetheart was so completely focused on protecting my family business that she wasn't thinking of herself.

Taking my coffee mug out to the backyard, I sat and stared at the trees for a while. There must be a way to make Claudia trust and believe in us. Even though her father was obviously scum. Even though she'd never had anyone to really rely on before.

She always seemed so strong and capable while she was at work, yet in private, I could see how vulnerable she was.

Then it clicked.

Women loved drama, if the few fragments I'd seen of those TV movies were to be believed. I'd have to resort to drastic measures. Ladies wanted grand gestures. Huge declarations of love.

Well, my darling wife was going to get one.

## 15

# CLAUDIA

Somehow I managed to maintain my focus just long enough to submit my final paper on Friday afternoon. I should have gone out to celebrate. But I couldn't. I felt lost.

By early Saturday evening, things were not improving. I'd nearly worn a groove in my living room carpet from pacing back and forth, my light blue sundress wrinkled from being balled up in my fists. I couldn't bring myself to go outside to enjoy the late sunshine. Everything that made me think of summer also made me think of Vaughan.

I didn't know what was worse, the possibility that I had embarrassed him, or that I might have hurt his business in some way. He acted casual most of the time, but I knew that the construction company was his baby. The most important thing in his life.

Although I'd barely been able to eat for days, I forced myself to nibble a granola bar before flopping onto the couch. Maybe I could find some old movie that would at least turn my mind off for a couple of hours.

Just as I picked up the remote, there was a tap at the door.

Sighing, I ran a hand through my hair as I went to answer it. Either Mrs. Rivero's niece was selling cookies again, or Sam from down the hall was going away for the weekend and wanted me to feed his cat.

I honestly never expected Vaughan to be on the other side of the door.

"Go away. You don't want to talk to me," I said, backing up.

He jammed his foot in the door, and carefully pushed it open. "Grab your purse and a sweater."

"What?"

"I'm taking you somewhere. Grab your stuff."

"I'm not going anywhere with you." I tried to wipe the smudges away from under my eyes, but Vaughan just smiled, taking my hand.

"If you refuse to talk to me, fine. I'm taking you somewhere where we can sit in silence."

He was being strangely pushy, which was so unlike him. But those dancing green eyes were extremely amused, making me want to smile along with him.

"And if I refuse?"

"Then this becomes a kidnapping," he shrugged. "I'm serious. I can easily throw you over my shoulder, Missy. Let's go."

I tied a sweater around my waist and grabbed my purse, locking the door behind me. Vaughan's hand gravitated to the center of my back to caress me gently, draining some of the tension from my shoulders. By the time we were in the truck, I had actually unclenched a bit.

"Why don't you put on some music," he suggested as he pulled out into the street. "Something mellow."

"What kind of lousy kidnapper lets the victim choose the music?" I giggled.

"I thought we weren't talking," he said, glancing with a raised eyebrow in a futile attempt to look sinister.

"Oh. Right." It was hard to keep a straight face when he was being so adorable.

I felt like I should be annoyed that he was forcing us to be together, but was secretly relieved that he was taking the lead. Yet I knew that things ultimately couldn't change between us. I wasn't good for him, and I was going to have to stay away. There had to be a clean break.

Maybe once he'd said his piece he would let me go.

We drove down toward the beach, and for a moment I thought he was going to take us to that lovely restaurant again. Instead, he turned and headed straight for the unfinished condo tower.

"What are we doing here?" I asked.

"We're being quiet."

I loved how his eyes sparkled with mirth. In a strange way, I loved how he was bringing us together without speaking. On top of his sweetness, why did he have to be so darn clever?

Vaughan led me into the lobby, which was finished, but unpainted. It was strange to see a building at this partial level of completion.

As we went into the elevator, I noticed that he pressed eighteen, even though the numbers went up to twenty-two.

"Anything higher than eighteen is still a hard hat area," he explained. "I don't want to take you anywhere that has open windows and equipment lying around."

"Okay."

We got off the elevator onto a floor that was nothing but walls, columns, and floor to ceiling windows. Vaughan wrapped an arm around me, guiding me around the block of walls for what would likely be washrooms.

"Oh," I gasped, as I looked through the wall of glass at the perfect sunset over the water. The colors melted into each other like an impressionist painting, so vivid and clear that I could barely bring myself to blink.

Vaughan's strong hands guided me to a bright blue rectangle on the bare concrete floor. As we got closer, I saw that it was an inflated camping mattress.

"Let's pretend it's a couch," he said as we sat down. There was a little white cooler beside him, and he opened the lid. "Champagne, ice cream, or both?"

"You've got to be kidding me."

"Nope." He held up an ice cream bar and a can.

"Canned champagne?"

"It's prosecco, but sure."

"Let's split them?" I suggested.

Vaughan cracked the can open and handed it to me, then divided the ice cream bar, handing me my half with a paper napkin. The combination of the two flavors was too sweet until the dark chocolate began to play with the bubbly wine. Then it was heaven.

"It's a little known scientific fact that people are unable to be stressed while eating ice cream, did you know that?."

He spread his legs, turning so that he could pull my back to his chest and shoulder so that I had something to lean on. I wasn't sure about the ice cream theory, but as soon as I felt his warmth, everything did seem a bit better.

"Vaughan, I—"

"No talking for a bit. Just eat, drink, and stare at the sky. Breathe."

"You're a pretty bossy kidnapper, you know," I giggled.

His arm tightened around me for a moment. "Shh."

We shared the wine and ice cream while watching the sky darken from peachy-pink to mauve. Then he set everything aside and wrapped his hands around my stomach.

Leaning against his chest, it was as if his calm, his strength, was flowing into me. As the waves far below lapped onto the shore and the few light clouds remaining turned purple, I felt like all of the tension had been drained from me.

If the point to this had been to chill me out enough to talk, it really did work. Yet nothing would change the fact that I wasn't good for him or his business. No matter what he said, I couldn't bring the toxic waste of my father into his life to poison everything.

"You're sweet for wanting to get me to a point where I can talk, but there's nothing to talk about," I said. "I'm not good enough for you. Being associated with my Dad will be bad for your business. You need to be with someone else."

A tear spilled down my cheek, which was infuriating. I wanted to sound firm.

Vaughan shook his head, then wiped away the tear with his thumb. Turning me back toward the window, he held me against his chest while lightly holding his hand over my mouth so I couldn't speak any more.

I wanted to laugh. I wanted him to kiss me and forget about everything else. But I couldn't let him spoil his successful family business just for me. No matter how I truly felt, I couldn't mess up his family's company.

# 16

## VAUGHAN

She was scared. I could feel it in the occasional trembles along her spine, and the way she just didn't want to listen to reason. Maybe growing up without having a father figure in her life had left Claudia unable to trust men. Or unable to feel secure.

I just needed to get her calm enough to hear me out.

Holding her snugly in my arms with my hand over her mouth, she stiffened for a moment, then relaxed against me.

If she truly wanted to leave, I'd release her in a heartbeat and take her home, of course. The turmoil in her eyes said that she was confused and unsure, but she wasn't afraid in the slightest.

"When the building is finished, this floor is actually going to be a restaurant on the other side, and a lounge on this side," I murmured into her ear. "Where we're sitting right now is going to be the dance floor area of a cocktail lounge."

"Hmm," she muttered with a nod.

"So I thought that having cocktails and ice cream here while lounging was a good idea."

Claudia's head swiveled as she looked up at me, then nodded. I released her mouth, turning her so that she snuggled into my shoulder.

"Just listen, baby," I said, stroking her back. "I don't know what you've heard about your father's Mayoral campaign, but the only people who are backing him are basically lowlifes. All of the people with actual power are putting their support behind Mayor Bennett to run another term. There's no way in hell that your Dad is going to win. From some of the rumors swirling around, he might even be forced to drop out of the race."

"Really?" she asked eagerly.

I placed a finger over her lips. "Silence, prisoner."

"Oops, right. Sorry."

"You have no idea how good you've already been for my business, Claudia. I have work lined up that is going to keep me busy for the next three months. I have requests for proposals that are going to fill the company's dance card until the middle of next year."

Claudia's beautiful blue eyes were wide as she mouthed the word, "Wow."

"The Oxfords are dying to have us come to their party, where there's going to be three directors of a wealth management company I've been dying to talk to. Instead of a formal meeting in a cold boardroom, which I hate, you and I can get to know them over burgers and beer." I paused. "Okay, with those people it's likely to be ultra rare whiskey and some kind of exotic bacon-wrapped fillet mignon. Whatever. The thing is, all of the wives adored you and want you in their social circle."

"Really?" Claudia's fingers fluttered to her throat, reminding me that her hand was bare. Strange how that nearly made my stomach turn over.

"I'm going to have to hire another assistant just to keep track of everything," I continued. "But I will cancel every event if that's what would make you happy. I just want you, Claudia. I need you in my life. I would sell the family business in a heartbeat if it meant that I could keep you."

"I would never ask you to do that," she whispered.

"I know, baby. I just need you to understand that you are the most important thing in my life. The fact that you happen to be incredible for business is simply a strangely wonderful fringe benefit. Even if you wanted to be with me without any of the corporate events, that would also be fine. Please, just tell me you're not going to give up on us."

My lips brushed against the top of her hair, then I tilted her back to stare into her eyes.

Her bottom lip quivered. "You're not worried that Dad's reputation is going to rub off on us?"

"Not at all. I've checked into it, and nobody is taking him seriously. They found out he has a criminal past. He ran several companies into the ground. The news of this is just starting to get around now. His entire reputation is destroyed, or about to be, and nobody knows that you're related to him."

"Jessica does," she said in a tiny voice.

"Jessica took a wild guess," I said, trying to chuckle to lighten the mood. "And what do you think her reputation is like? She dresses like a deranged prom queen, talks too loudly while openly insulting people, and basically burns bridges everywhere she goes. Trust me – not a single corporate wife would ever invite her anywhere. I seriously doubt we'll ever run into her again."

I brushed my lips against Claudia's forehead. "I want to thank you again for making sure she stopped calling. Jessica will finally stop annoying me. I really appreciate that."

"So if she does say anything, they won't believe her?"

"Absolutely not. And there is no online connection anywhere between you and your father."

"You checked up on me," she smiled.

"Yes, I did. Just to prove to you that everything is absolutely fine."

Claudia's eyes shone up at me. "Thank you."

"We sort of did things out of order by playing husband and wife without really dating," I said slowly. "But there's no reason why we can't go back to the beginning. Let's just date. Hang out." I gestured around the echoing bare-bones space we were sitting in. "Let's lounge a bit more."

"Except at parties where we have to pretend to be married." Her fingers began to fiddle with the edge of my shirt.

I shrugged, shaking her in the process to make her smile. "We're so good at it. And Mom's ring looks great on you. Would you mind?"

"Not in the slightest," she said. "But somebody is going to eventually find out, don't you think?"

I shook my head, swinging her from side to side with me. "From the brilliant way you described our wedding, there wouldn't be a lot of photos online. People honestly don't poke into each other's lives very much unless there is something they're after. But all people want from us are amusing party anecdotes and buildings that are built faster and better than the competition."

Her teeth burrowed into her perfect bottom lip, still looking worried. Leaning in, I nuzzled just under her ear. "Please, Claudia. I need you. I've never needed anyone as much as I need you. There's something about you that just makes everything feel right."

I felt her body move in waves as she took a few slow

deep breaths. It felt like my entire future was hanging in the balance.

"I'll never abandon you like he did, baby," I whispered.

Cupping her face in my hands, I kissed her forehead. "I love you, Claudia. I'd marry you tomorrow, but I know you're going to want us to take some time first. I want us to be a team. Forever. We belong together. I know it, and I know you know it."

All I could do was wait, the space between every heartbeat seeming to take forever.

**17**

---

**CLAUDIA**

Vaughan was simply amazing. Any other man would have simply tossed me to the curb for being so irrational. Or at least, corrected me in a way that made me feel terrible.

But he'd actually taken the time to relax me so that I could listen to him properly and take it all in. More than anything else, that told me that he was the one. He was prepared to be patient with me.

All I had to do was let my guard down, and let him in.

Holding back a laugh, I asked myself what "Claudia the waitress" would do in this situation. She would either blame everything on Scotty, to make everyone laugh. Or she would throw a hand on one hip and say something saucy, pretending that she had been right all along. But neither of those felt right in this situation.

Maybe now I could do the right thing by simply being me, and being honest.

"Vaughan, it means a lot to me that you went to all this trouble to check up on my father, and that you still want to be with me."

"Of course, sweetheart—"

I held a finger over his lips. "Please, let me spit this out."

He nodded, stroking my back gently, making me melt against him.

"My mother was unbelievably quiet, so she never stopped Dad when he was being ridiculous, or when he took off on us. I always worried that if I was that quiet and shy, people would take off on me as well."

Vaughan nodded as if he wanted me to continue.

"So I've been trying to be more outgoing. Over the past year, I've forced myself to be bubbly and bright at work. I always told myself it was to make better tips, but really, it was testing what being more confident would feel like."

He smiled, nodding again.

"But as I've been trying to break out of my shell, it's been uneven. I think that's why I panicked so terribly at the thought of you knowing what a scumbag my father is. Knowing that I was related to such a lowlife. I thought that might make you think I wasn't good enough to be with you."

Vaughan's mouth fell open, then he crushed me against his chest in a bear hug. "Oh, baby, no. No. Please don't think that for one second. You're the most amazing person I've ever met."

He tilted my head to kiss me, slow and sultry, with that gathering steam that drove me wild. Just as my fingers began running through the back of his hair, he pulled away.

"To be honest, it did feel like you were acting now and then. I wasn't sure whether it was to please me, or just because you were nervous. Maybe I can help you if it's the second one."

I'd do anything he asked as long as he kept rubbing my back, taking hold of me so possessively.

"Claudia, if you're always open with me about how

you're really feeling, I can give you as much space, or as much support as you need on any given day. It doesn't have to be even. Growth is always messy, right?"

"How on earth did I get so lucky?" I laughed, curling into his shoulder again.

Then I straightened up to hold his face in my hands. "I love you, Vaughan. Yes, we're a team. Forever." I kissed him gently before adding, "And yeah, a real wedding should probably wait for at least a little bit."

"We can wait for however long you want. Everything is your speed from now on, baby. I just want you to be open with me. Always."

"Always," I answered, smiling.

Vaughan laid back across the weird plastic mattress, nudging the cooler out of the way as he stretched out and pulled me on top of him.

I don't know why getting everything out in the open felt so cleansing, but it was as if my entire body and soul were refreshed.

Then aroused. Every single one of Vaughan's inhalations moved me against his body, reminding me of what was just under my skirt and his jeans. Suddenly every inch of my skin felt like it was melting from the heat between us.

Vaughan was so huge, so firm and broad, that I felt tiny on top of him. I also strangely felt like I was in control, which was weirdly erotic. Rubbing myself against him, I watched his eyes grow wide.

"What do you think you're up to?" he asked.

I glanced around at the steel frames and bare drywall. "There aren't any security cameras in here yet, right?"

He nuzzled my throat, dragging his teeth along my skin to make me squeal. "No, you naughty girl. Are you trying to tell me that you need something?"

"Yes."

His huge rough hands slipped up the back of my thighs and under my skirt, and tore my panties off.

"I'll buy you more," he growled as he kissed a path to my ear. His tongue dragged along the shell, the sound of his ragged breath making me feel needy and frantic.

I could feel the clenching of tiny muscles I didn't even know I had until the night we had spent together playing man and wife. But it wasn't a game anymore. It was just a matter of time, as we did things out of order.

Vaughan unbuttoned the front of my dress and pushed down my bra so that he could take my already hard nipple into his mouth. I loved that he wasn't being aggressive, just...urgent.

Before I even realized what he was doing, his jeans were unzipped and hitched down.

"Tell me you want me," he rumbled against my skin.

"I want you. You know I do." Our voices sounded strange in this echoey place with nothing but a concrete floor.

I reached down to take his erection in my hand, stroking him gently as Vaughan's eyes almost rolled back into his head. "Baby, you have no idea..."

I loved how strained his voice sounded with his back teeth clamping together as he gripped my hips, moving my body against him.

I could barely breathe, fondling his rigid length as I got into position over him. Lifting up, I dragged the thick head through my folds, shocked at how wet I was. I had barely slipped him inside me when I felt those thick fingers dig into my hips, holding me motionless.

"We are never going to doubt each other again, are we?" he asked.

I shook my head. "No."

"You believe in us? You understand that we're forever?"

I nodded eagerly. Then he released me so that I could concentrate on slowly sinking down, spreading my legs wider as his hard, thick cock filled me completely.

When I couldn't lower myself any further, Vaughan took hold of me, pulling my lips to his as he began to rock up into me with deep, powerful thrusts.

"So gorgeous," he rasped. "My sweet, sexy girl."

He sounded so hungry, as if he were barely in control. Knowing that I thrilled him this much was almost impossible to believe. But it was true. Somehow Vaughan was just as head over heels for me as I was for him.

We moved steadily faster as his huge cock filled me over and over. I couldn't believe that anything could feel so good.

"I love you," I managed to gasp as I looked down into those magical green eyes.

"I love you too, baby. So much."

Vaughan buried himself inside me, deeper and faster as I found the angle that dragged him across my swollen clit.

How strange that my entire sex life would begin and end with this incredible man, I suddenly thought. Strangely, that excited me in a way that felt wildly special.

Even though my skirt was covering us well enough, if anyone happened to walk in, there would have been no mistaking what was going on. Yet I didn't care. Right now, I couldn't have stopped for anything.

Vaughan gripped my outer thigh with one hand in the back of my neck with the other, holding me against him tightly. "Baby," he choked, "you feel so perfect. I think I'm already addicted to your cute little noises."

I nearly giggled, but it turned into a long, low sigh as I felt the pressure swirling like a tornado deep inside me. His hips moved faster, driving his length up into me deeper and deeper. It felt like we were both possessed by the intensity of this moment.

Everything was so fast, yet so right. Just like us. Vaughan knew how to work my body perfectly, applying pressure, balancing my weight, as if my orgasm was his only focus.

"Yes..." I moaned as my body began to tighten around him. Clinging to him desperately, I could both feel and hear the deep sucking sounds with every thrust.

"Claudia, baby," Vaughan murmured, kissing me deeply, then catching my eyes. "My angel. My precious girl."

My head fell back with a scream that echoed off the glass and concrete, the climax ripping from my body as I bucked up and down wildly. Grinding down against him, my writhing seemed to fill him with another wave of passion.

His hands gripped me almost roughly, holding me in place. He tried to speak, but it dissolved into a grunting moan as I felt his hot seed fill me in long, wet bursts.

I collapsed on top of him, and Vaughan stroked my back gently, rocking me in his arms. "I didn't know that you were such a wild woman," he whispered. "See? I'm learning about all of your different personalities."

Laughing, I tried to get up but my hips were stiff and sore from the strange position. Vaughan shifted me to the side, then started to pull his pants back on. He reached into the pocket then grabbed my hand.

Slipping the emerald and diamond ring back on my finger, he said, "I never want to see you without this again. Unless I replace it with a bigger ring someday."

"Or if I'm teaching you how to garden," I laughed. "I'm going to teach you how to choose plants and green up that big backyard."

"Yes, dear."

He kissed me in a butterfly-soft caress, telling me that pretending to be hen-pecked was going to be his running gag. I already knew that I was going to laugh with him every single time.

# EPILOGUE ONE
## VAUGHAN


** Three Months Later **

I honestly had no idea if Claudia would guess what I was up to, but I had to try for the surprise anyway.

Running a cloth around the base of the new lamp, I shifted it into place then went to break down the delivery boxes. I had insisted that Claudia start putting her touch on the house. Not just so that it looked like a woman lived here, but so that she would be comfortable.

Now that we'd been together for three months, it was annoying for her to keep her apartment when she stayed with me so often, especially since we had at least two functions a week where we had to dress up.

I loved the way we both pretended to gripe and complain about the elegant affairs, yet always had the best time at them. Claudia's dress sales lady Jeanette had resorted to simply pulling dresses she knew would be perfect, and now they had a monthly shopping date where my sweetheart made her final choices.

Claudia had transformed into the ultimate corporate wife without even realizing it.

She kept tabs on all of the other women, and was constantly sending notes of encouragement when they had a big project coming up at work, or when one of their kids had an important soccer game. Every time we found a new restaurant, there were five new friends who had to hear about it.

She was absolutely thriving.

Her new job was amazing, and she completely lit up when she told me about the projects she was working on. She had already been bringing new business into the PR company with all of her new top tier corporate contacts, and they loved her for it.

In short, my darling girlfriend was a dynamo and I couldn't be more proud.

Well, I could. In just a few more minutes.

Finally I heard Claudia's new car in the driveway. Since I couldn't always pick her up from work and the bus wasted a lot of time, last month I insisted on getting her a safe, reliable car. She pretended to protest, but I could tell that she was extremely relieved. I threatened to kidnap her again to take her to the auto dealer if she wouldn't come on her own.

I also had to abduct her to take her to a couple of furniture stores so she could pick out a couch that wasn't "apparently made of rock".

"Hey, honey," Claudia's sweet voice rang out as she came into the foyer. She set a few bags down, then turned to where I was sitting on the brand new living room couch.

"Oh my god!" she squealed. "It looks even better in here than I imagined. Plus you have the lamp in the perfect spot."

"Anything for my gorgeous wife," I teased, pulling her down to sit beside me. "How was your day?"

"Unbelievable. Ellen needs PR for three of the charities she works with, and they're all hiring us. I'm already up for a promotion in a few months, but I'm going to be managing one of her accounts right away."

"That's because you're amazing," I said as I nuzzled her throat. "Even though you work too hard sometimes."

Claudia laughed. "At least I'm not on my feet slinging burgers all night. I loved the people at the diner, but it was really rough on the feet."

"We should have dinner there next week so that you can order something ridiculous that's not on the menu to freak Scotty out."

"Great idea, I love it!" she exclaimed.

It was so wonderful to see her so relaxed that I almost didn't want to get her all excited again. Yet I couldn't possibly wait another moment.

"Let me show you the closet." Taking her hand, I led her upstairs. "I called Jeanette to have her ship over another ten cocktail dresses and matching shoes."

"Oh my God, you didn't!" Claudia laughed. "I mean, thank you, husband."

We went into the bedroom, then the closet, where I'd cleared a huge section for her things even before she had moved in.

She followed my pointing finger toward the new dresses, and racks of shoes. Then I opened a drawer. "Necklaces and bracelets."

"Wow," she breathed. "Thank you."

Opening the top drawer, I said, "Dangly earrings for parties. Oh, and there's one more pair. Here."

Dropping to one knee, I held up a small box. Claudia's hand flew to her mouth as she gasped. The one-carat diamond studs were perfectly classic. Below them was a ring.

"Mom wants you to keep her ring. I'd like to add this as a wedding band," I said, taking hold of her shaking hand. It was a row of alternating diamonds and emeralds that complemented my mother's piece perfectly. Slipping it on her finger, it looked absolutely perfect.

"Claudia, will you marry me?"

She nodded quickly, sniffling slightly as her eyes became glassy. "Yes."

I stood up to kiss her, soft and deep, possessing those lips that I'd grown to crave every minute of every day.

Lifting her slightly, I danced her awkwardly out of the walk-in closet, then down the hall to the guest room that had become my odds and ends junk room.

As I opened the door, Claudia froze. The room was completely empty except for a purple teddy bear sitting on the center of the cream carpet, on a little pillow that I'd borrowed from an easy chair in the basement.

"A teddy bear requires a seat?" she asked, clutching my arm.

"Well, yeah. I didn't want him to sit on the floor. He'd look sad. I want him to be happy while he waits to meet our kids someday."

Claudia's bottom lip was quivering, as she wiped away a tear. Then she nodded slowly.

"I want to make all the room for you that you need in this house," I said, holding her tightly. "But I'm also making room for everything that's coming along the way. Whenever that is."

"We should probably get legally married before we have kids," she said, looking up at me with a saucy smile. "And who knows how long it will take to plan a wedding."

"Twenty-two people by a lake in Vermont? That shouldn't take too long to pull together. Honestly, I think you've planned the entire wedding already."

Claudia's light laugh was one of my favorite sounds in the world. "You're okay with that?"

"Of course. It sounds simple, down-to-earth, and actually a lot of fun. Unless you wanted something glamorous?"

She shook her head empathetically. "No. Trust me, with the amount of time I spend in heels, I would much rather be in sneakers or hiking boots for most of my wedding day."

"There's one more little surprise," I said, pulling her into the next room which I used as my home office.

Flipping the laptop open, I waited as she read the invitation on the screen. It was for her birthday party next month, at the glamorous Thornton Hotel.

"Wow," she breathed. "Seriously?"

"We can change the venue if you want, and have any theme you like. But I thought since having an engagement party might be...unusual, given the circumstances, we could have an engagement party disguised for everyone else as your birthday bash."

She fell against me, howling with laughter. "You sneaky man," she sputtered. "That is brilliant."

"My parents can meet you and your mother at your birthday party. Then we can have the wedding in the spring."

Even though Mom and Dad had only met Claudia through video calls so far, they absolutely adored her. Mom had taken to texting her every Sunday afternoon to hear all about how her week was going. At first, I was worried that Claudia might be annoyed by the intrusion, but instead she seemed genuinely touched that Mom was so interested in every detail of her life.

I also noticed that she had struggled to fight back tears when my dad was giving her advice about the car, and insisting that she call him with any questions at all.

"You've just thought of everything, haven't you," she said, stretching her arms up to wrap around my neck.

"I try. I need to keep impressing you enough to deserve you, my gorgeous girl."

Claudia stared at me for a moment, but instead of speaking, she brought her mouth to mine. Somehow she always managed to tell me exactly what she was thinking whenever she kissed me.

"I love you," I murmured against her lips.

"I love you too, husband and fiancé at the same time," she giggled.

Even though the timing of our relationship was messed up and convoluted, it didn't matter to me, as long as I had this wonderful girl with me.

"You don't mind that we've done everything ass-backward and out of order?" I asked, walking her back to our bedroom.

"Not at all. We were sort of semi-married before we had sex for the first time. Some people would consider that the height of propriety."

"I'm pretty sure I fell in love with you when I watched your eyes light up while describing our wedding," I said, untucking her shirt so that I could run my hands up her back.

"I'm pretty sure I fell in love with you the first time you kidnapped me." Her hands gripped my shoulders, pulling me down so that she could kiss the nook between my neck and shoulder.

Slipping each other's clothing off was a slow, seductive ritual that I was so grateful to experience almost every day.

Sometimes more frequently. We were always ravenous for each other.

No matter how connected we were, and how much we talked, our bodies always needed a deeper connection. It seemed to keep our minds perfectly in tune, no matter what was going on with our busy lives.

# EPILOGUE TWO
## CLAUDIA

** Six Years Later **

It was almost impossible to comprehend how much my life had changed over the past several years. Not a day went by that I wasn't incredibly grateful to my somewhat shy self for stepping up.

Somehow I had managed to turn my much bolder "Claudia the waitress" persona into a part of my everyday self. Which enabled me to go on a date with Vaughan, pretending to be his wife. Which led to networking with the city's elite, garnering tons of clients, and to promotions at lightning speed.

Not to mention, an engagement party disguised as a birthday soirée and the perfect romantic relaxed wedding. Sure, we had done some things in an unusual way. But it was our way, and that's all that mattered.

Tiptoeing towards the bright yellow bedroom, the door was wide open so I could peer through and see Vaughan sitting on the floor supervising while Nora stacked her blocks into a rather precarious tower. She was already wearing her purple flowered nightgown but didn't look the slightest bit sleepy.

"Remember, sweetie," Vaughan said softly, "all of the weight pushes down. So if you're going to go up, the base has to be stronger."

"Oh. Yeah." She added reinforcements around the bottom, then spread out the base slightly so that her tower stopped wobbling.

Only my husband could teach a four-year-old basic construction techniques and make it seem like they were just playing with blocks.

"Hey, baby," he said to me as he saw me in the doorway. "Why don't you go run a bath, and I'll put somebody—" he jerked his thumb right at Nora's tummy until she giggled, "to bed."

I swooped in to pick Nora up, bouncing little kisses all over her face until she was laughing hysterically. "Good night, sweet pea," I said, handing her to Vaughan.

"Night, Mommy."

I went back to our room, curling up with a cup of peppermint tea and the latest spy thriller that I had just begun. Vaughan often asked me why I read such things, worried that it was a sign that I needed more excitement in my life.

But with all my secret identities – glamorous corporate wife, PR writer, loving mother – I certainly had as much excitement in our lives as I'd ever wanted. Which is to say, as little as possible.

Although I couldn't hear the words of the story Nora was being read, I could hear Vaughan's deep voice rumble when he played the part of the big bad wolf.

"Hey, baby, why aren't you in the bath yet?"

My head jumped up and I almost dropped my e-reader,

realizing that I had drifted so far into the story that I'd lost track of time. Setting it aside, I patted the spot beside me on the bed.

"I'm really into this book," I said. "Plus, we're going to have to be careful when we take baths together for the next little while."

"Why?"

Staring into those brilliant green eyes, I had to choke back tears, knowing what his reaction was going to be.

"Baby, what's wrong?"

"You like them seriously hot. I can't take long, super hot baths, or go in hot tubs for the next nine months," I said, nodding slowly as I stared at him.

Vaughan froze, not even blinking for three straight seconds. Then he lunged, grabbing me, wrapping me in his arms as he showered me with kisses.

"Another baby?"

"Yes," I managed to choke through my tears.

"I love you," he said, over and over. "I'm so excited. I love you."

"And I love you," I said. "You're ready for another round of midnight feedings and endless diapers?"

Vaughan pulled away to clasp our hands between us. "It wasn't nearly as terrible as people warned us."

"That's likely because you hired help immediately," I laughed.

Vaughan had been so concerned that I would be overworked and stressed that the second we found out I was pregnant for the first time, he hired a cleaning lady to come three times a week, and then a professional nanny to help us set up the baby's room, and assist me with every single part of the transition to motherhood.

Basically, I was completely spoiled rotten.

"Who knows?" I said with a smirk. "Maybe the first child is the easy one, and the second one will be a holy terror."

"Then we'll hand him over to Taylor to babysit now and then," Vaughan chuckled.

Taylor, Bob, and some of the other guys from Vaughan's best crew had already built a huge jungle gym play set in the backyard, complete with a gazebo.

"I can't imagine what you guys are going to build if the second one is a boy," I laughed.

I reached for a tissue to dab the tears from my eyes, and by the time I looked back, Vaughan was naked. He slipped under the covers, sliding my nightgown off without words.

As we made love gently, I could feel his hunger take on the same intensity as it had when I was pregnant with Nora. It was beautiful to know that he was just as attracted to me as ever. But when I was pregnant, his lust was deeper, more primal.

His sweet but slightly obsessive nature made me feel absolutely safe, especially now that it was more than just us.

I had known that we belonged together from the first time he dropped to his knees to ask me for a strange date. Now that our lives were completely intertwined, I could barely remember what the world was like before he caught me as I was about to fall down in the back of Ray's Diner.

Before I fell in love with the most incredible man in the world, and learned that I didn't need to change my personality in order to be good enough for him, or anyone else.

~

You'll also enjoy:
Fake Summer Boyfriend
Fake Summer Husband

# ALSO BY HALEY TRAVIS

## Her New Bodyguard: Jackson

Ashley was so sexy and innocent that my need to care for her was far more than professional.

## Never Date The Boss

Ashley was talked into one little "business date" with her boss, and everything changed in a heartbeat. Or rather, a flutter of them.

## Never Kiss The Boss

One little drink. One little party night with the girls. One huge mystery man and a heart-flipping makeout session. Then one giant, sexy problem...

## Mr. Right... As Rain

A gorgeous man saved me on the way to an interview. Maybe it was the good luck kiss from a stranger, but isn't falling in love so fast just a fantasy?

## Mr. Right... Before Your Eyes

Finn seemed instantly obsessed with me. His desire was an awakening, lighting a fire inside me. Should I listen to my anxiety or my newly ignited libido?

## The Last Date

I was infatuated with Sasha. I will tease her, even court her, until I make her mine. Forever.

**Teased by my Roommate**

A new roommate named Hawk. He's breathtaking, sexy, and I've already seen FAR too much of him. Now he'll never stop teasing me. But I love it.

### Daddy's Billionaire Lawyer

Just a few stolen kisses with a sexy masked man in the rose garden. I would never have expected to start a relationship with a hot billionaire.

### Daddy's Billionaire Boss

When Emily discovers her Dad's boss is the improbable man her aunt predicted she'd fall for, can she fit into his world?

**Mackton Mechanics** *(3 part series coming Fall 2022)*

*Rev your engines and get ready for these hot alpha men!*

These mechanics are comfortable working with steel. What will happen when they're tinkering with a sweet girl's heart instead of an engine?

Please join the mailing list at

www.haleytravisromance.com

for new releases, updates, discounts & freebies!

9 798844 053573